BLADE
PLAYING DEAD

PLAYING DEAD

tim
bowler

philomel books/penguin young readers group

Originally published in the United Kingdom by Oxford University Press.
First American Edition published 2009 by PHILOMEL BOOKS. A division of Penguin Young Readers Group. Published by The Penguin Group. Penguin Group (USA) Inc., 375 Hudson Street, New York, NY 10014, U.S.A. Penguin Group (Canada), 90 Eglinton Avenue East, Suite 700, Toronto, Ontario M4P 2Y3, Canada (a division of Pearson Penguin Canada Inc.). Penguin Books Ltd, 80 Strand, London WC2R 0RL, England. Penguin Ireland, 25 St. Stephen's Green, Dublin 2, Ireland (a division of Penguin Books Ltd). Penguin Group (Australia), 250 Camberwell Road, Camberwell, Victoria 3124, Australia (a division of Pearson Australia Group Pty Ltd). Penguin Books India Pvt Ltd, 11 Community Centre, Panchsheel Park, New Delhi—110 017, India. Penguin Group (NZ), 67 Apollo Drive, Rosedale, North Shore 0632, New Zealand (a division of Pearson New Zealand Ltd). Penguin Books (South Africa) (Pty) Ltd, 24 Sturdee Avenue, Rosebank, Johannesburg 2196, South Africa. Penguin Books Ltd, Registered Offices: 80 Strand, London WC2R 0RL, England.

Printed in the United States of America.
Design by Richard Amari.
Text set in Charlotte Book.

Library of Congress Cataloging-in-Publication Data
Bowler, Tim. Blade : playing dead / Tim Bowler.—1st American ed. p. cm. Summary: A fourteen-year-old British street person with extraordinary powers of observation and self-control must face murderous thugs connected with a past he has tried to forget, when his skills with a knife earned him the nickname Blade. [1. Street children—Fiction. 2. Violence—Fiction. 3. Murder—Fiction. 4. Gangs—Fiction. 5. Homeless persons—Fiction. 6. England—Fiction.] I. Title. PZ7.B6786Bl 2009 [Fic]—dc22 2008037813.

ISBN 978-0-399-25186-3
10 9 8 7 6 5 4 3 2 1

For Rachel
with my love

BLADE
PLAYING DEAD

1

So he's looking at me with his puggy face, this big jerk of a policeman, and I'm thinking, take him out or let him live?

Big question.

I don't like questions. Questions are about choices and choices are a pain. I like certainties. Got to do this, got to do that, no debate. Take him out, let him live. Know what you got to do. Certainty.

Only I'm not certain here. I'm pretty sure I want to take him out. I hate the sight of him and I hate being back at the police station.

The knife feels good hidden inside my sock. Pugface didn't even feel it when he frisked me. But he'll feel it pretty quick if he doesn't treat me right. It's only a small blade but I know how to use it.

He's still watching me with those pig eyes.

"Right, young man," he says.

"I'm not your young man."

He takes no notice. He's too busy smirking.

"In your own words," he goes on.

"In your own words what?"

"In your own words—what happened?"

"What happened where?"

He gives this heavy, exaggerated sigh. I hate that. Move my fingers slowly down my thigh.

He can't see with the desk in the way. That bosomy police-woman over by the door's watching but she can't see anything either. I can tell from her face.

Anyway, she's too far away. I can have my knife out and into Pugface before she's covered half the ground between us. Probably time to stick her too.

He goes on in that patronizing voice.

"What happened at the pedestrian crossing?"

My fingers are close to the knife now. I stop my hand. No need to move it any farther. I'm safe enough. All that's needed is a lunge and a thrust. Maybe a bit more if Bosoms gets involved.

"What happened at the crossing?" says Pugface.

"Nothing."

"You stood in the road after the lights had turned to green and refused to move and let the traffic pass."

"Did I?"

"You shouted abuse at the drivers waiting to move on."

"Can't remember."

"Especially the man in the nearest car."

"Can't remember."

"The man in the green station wagon. He asked you to move aside so that he and everybody else could drive on. You swore back at him and made obscene gestures."

"He was rude to me."

"You don't think maybe you were the one being rude?"

I shrug. I'm starting to enjoy this now.

"Eh?" says Pugface.

"Don't know."

"It was dangerous."

"No, it wasn't. He was never going to run me over."

"Because unlike you, he had some sense of responsibility. Though it would have shaken you up quite a bit if he had put his foot down and driven at you. I don't doubt you'd have moved aside pretty quickly if he'd done that."

"He wouldn't have had the guts."

"Is that what you think stopped him? Lack of guts?"

"Yeah."

"That's what you'd have done, is it? If you'd been the driver and you'd seen some rude little kid standing on the crossing and refusing to move? Jeering and swearing at you, and daring you to drive on? You'd have put your foot down and run him over, would you?"

"Too right."

He leans back in the chair, glances at Bosoms. I'm really having fun now. They're both out of their depth. They don't know what to do with me. They know they can't prosecute or anything. It's just not that big a deal. I'll get a warning, nothing more.

Then Pugface stands up.

"Seems like we've got a problem, then."

He moves around the desk toward me. I don't like the look of him suddenly. Don't know why. He sits on the edge of the desk.

Too close. Don't like people that close. Makes me remember things. I think of the knife, squeeze my hands into a ball. He glances at Bosoms again, then back at me.

"The driver's told us he doesn't wish to take things further. He just wanted to report the incident."

Say nothing.

"He was a bit worried we might not be able to trace the boy who held up the traffic for five minutes, swore at all the drivers, then ran off." Pugface sniffs. "He clearly wasn't aware just how well we know you around here."

He leans closer. I'm hating this now. It's not the police station. It's this face leering down at me. He's got to pull back. He's got to do it now, right now.

But he doesn't. He just smirks again—then leans even closer.

"Do you really think," he whispers, "that we haven't noticed you've got something hidden inside your sock?"

I lunge for the knife—in vain. The man's hands are tight around my arms. I don't even see the woman move. One minute she's over by the door, the next she's behind me, pulling me back against the chair. I spit at 'em, snarl at 'em, try to break free. Doesn't do any good.

"Bastards!" I'm rocking about, screaming my head off. "Bloody bastards!"

"Yeah, yeah," says Pugface. "Bloody bastards."

"Got a nice tongue on him," says the woman.

"Bastards!" I scream.

"Look inside his sock," mutters the policeman.

The woman pulls out the knife, fumbles with the other sock.

"There's nothing in there," I yell.

She checks anyway, then straightens up, holding the knife. The man lets go of me and takes it from her. I duck under their arms and make a dash for the door.

I'm not fast—no point pretending—but being small sometimes helps, and somehow I've taken 'em by surprise. I'm at the door before 'em. I can see Pugface's hands clutching at me, and the woman's, but they're kind of falling over each other.

Then I'm out in the corridor.

Shouts from inside the room. Some constable running toward me from the desk. That's when fire extinguishers come in handy. A squirt over the guy and he slips. Jump over him and out the door.

Nothing to it.

2

AND THAT WAS when I was seven.

Now that I've turned fourteen, I look back and you know what's weird? It's like nothing's changed. I still don't like the police and I still don't like people getting close.

And that includes you, Bigeyes.

Not quite sure why I'm talking to you at all. I don't even know you. Maybe it's something Becky said to me. You got to make sense of your life. You got to think about what you're doing. You got to think before you act. And if you ever want to talk, I'm here for you.

Except Becky's dead.

So maybe that's why I'm dumping on you.

Not that I feel obliged to tell you the truth, mind. Don't get any ideas. I mean, I might tell you the truth but I might not. Just so you know.

I call the shots here. I choose what I say and what I don't. You can choose whether to stay or wig it somewhere else. And if you choose to wig it, that's fine with me. I don't need you. Remember that.

I don't need anyone.

Thing about lying—we're all told it's wrong. Tell the truth, tell the truth, tell the truth. But where's that ever got anyone? I've been lying since as long as I can remember. Why? Cos everyone I've ever known has lied to me.

So what am I going to tell you? Not much, so don't get

excited. You probably want to know my name. Well, that's a bit of a problem. I got loads.

There's the name I was given as a baby, but that's a dronky name, so I never use it. Then there's the names I make up. I got garbage bags of those. Different names for different people. Depends on where I am and who I'm with.

But there is one name I like.

It's the name Becky gave me. A name from the past. Everybody called me it in the old days. No one does now cos no one in this city knows it. And that's fine. I don't like to remember. But I do like the name. You can use it if you want.

BLADE.

That's what they used to call me. And I liked it. Bit of style, bit of clash. But remember—it's a secret. Don't be a clap-head and spew it. If I find out you've blotched on me, then you'll find out why Becky called me Blade.

As for the rest of the world, I don't give two bells what people call me. Why fuss about a name when you can make 'em up so easy? And you know what? Life's a bit like that too.

Easy, simple, no sweat.

What you shaking your head for? Don't believe me? Well, I don't care. Believe what you like. It's true anyway. Life's a whack. It's no big deal coping with stuff. Other people—they make a horse trough out of it, get stressed out. Me, I'm different.

It's like I'm on top of this mountain, this great big mountain, higher than all the others, higher than—what's it called?—Everest. Miles higher. I'm all on my own with my head way up above everybody else, and I'm fine about it.

There's no one'll ever conquer me, cos no one'll ever get near me.

You listening to this, Bigeyes?

That's what it's about. It's about seeing things from a higher place than everybody else. Seeing things no one else can.

Like that guy in Café Blue Sox. I can see things about him no one else can. I can see things about him even he can't see. Got him? Table by the window. Not the guy with the vomity hair. He'll be leaving in a minute. Don't ask me how I know.

The other guy, the one with the mobile phone. Brown hair, about twenty, bit smooth. Got him?

There's loads like him around here. Big head, small brain. This city breeds 'em. Very easy meat. He'll finish his phone call in a minute, drape his coat over the back of that empty chair next to him and forget about it.

Why? Cos all his attention'll be taken up with that blond girl behind the bar.

There you go. What did I tell you? Vomity's leaving. Now—watch Dogbrain. There he goes, see? Mobile down, sip of coffee, coat over the chair.

Walk over, stand outside, wander in. Busy place, lots of yak. Even better.

No one notices me. I'm good at that. No one notices me when I don't want 'em to. I might be invisible. Only the red-lipped girl behind the bar sees me, and that's just cos I want a coffee.

Blondie's already over by the window talking to Dogbrain.

"Can I help you?" says Redlips.

"Latte, please. Medium."

She fixes me the latte. Take it over to the window. Blondie's still there, leaning over the guy's chair. They're talking about nothing. Murmurs, giggles.

Sit down at the next table. They don't notice. Move the chair closer to his. More murmurs, giggles. They're talking about a guy he knows, some dungpot called Kenny.

Check around me, check the guy, check the girl.

Nobody even knows I'm here. I might be a dream, a spirit. I love doing this. I know where the wallet is. I can see the shape of it from here. Inside pocket of the jacket, closed with a zip.

Another check around—stop. Blondie's straightened up. She's looking me over. But she's not noticing me. She's thinking of Dogbrain even as she looks at me.

The guy hasn't even turned. He's drinking her up with his eyes like she's some kind of cocktail. She looks back at him, leans down again, puts a hand on his shoulder.

Two minutes later I've drunk my latte and gone. And I've got a nice fat wallet.

I've also got a problem.

I'm being followed.

3

CAN'T SEE ANYONE but someone's after me. Don't ask me how I know.

Keep a lookout, Bigeyes.

It's not Dogbrain. I know that much. It's no one from Café Blue Sox. It's someone else. More than one person too. I can feel eyes on me from several places. Don't distract me. I need to work out how many people there are.

Four at least. Maybe more. Hard to tell.

Look behind. Check the High Street.

Nobody. Nobody dangerous anyway. Lots of people but they're all muffins.

Walk on.

Two men, big hairy gobbos like they're off a building site. It's not them. Another gobbo coming the other way. But he's running for a bus.

Danger's still there. I can feel it. Which way? Left or right? Never mind, I'll decide. Left, down to the end of Crowstone Road, right at the bottom, down the pedestrian precinct.

Walk, walk, walk.

Still don't feel right. There's definitely more than four people. I can feel at least five, maybe more.

Glance around.

Nobody.

Walk on. End of the precinct, down the alleyway, hurry through it to Meadway Drive, on toward the canal. Don't run. They'll think I'm scared. Just keep walking, fast. Still a few people around but they're thinning out.

The canal looks quiet and the towpath's deserted. Not a good place to go but I can maybe cut across one of the bridges farther down and shake 'em off around the industrial estate.

It's a mistake. I know it the moment I set off down the towpath. Three figures in front of me. Trixi and two mates. If they've been following, they must have raced ahead and climbed over the fence. So where are the rest?

Look behind.

Three more covering my escape.

Shit, this is bad. Don't let anyone tell you girl gangs are a softer touch than boy gangs. They're worse. They fight dirty. And here's me with no weapon.

Trixi gives me a mocking little call.

"Hey, Slicky!"

They move in. I look about me. Canal on the left, fence on the right. Nothing for it. I make a dash for the fence.

But they catch me easy.

You can't fight six of 'em. I wouldn't want to take on one of 'em. Not these trolls. Boy gangs are another thing. There's always one or two muffins in there you can have a go at. Not this lot. You don't even get in the gang unless you've proved yourself and done some serious damage.

"Pull him back!" says Trixi.

They pull me back, throw me down on the towpath.

"Silly boy," she says, looking down.

"Trix. Lay off me."

"What you got?"

"Nothing."

I look up at the faces. Flint eyes, flint hearts. I don't even want to know what they're carrying.

"I got nothing, Trix."

"Stupid kid."

Say nothing. Let her call me a kid. She's older anyway. They're all about sixteen. She can call me a kid.

"Stupid kid," she says again.

"I got nothing, Trix."

"No wallet?"

"No."

She kicks me hard in the ribs.

"Ow!"

"No wallet?" she says.

It's stupid holding out. They're going to take everything anyway.

"Listen, Trix, I—"

"Check his pockets," she says.

They poke about, pull everything out.

"What a surprise," says Trixi. She holds up Dogbrain's wallet. "What else has he got?"

"Another wallet," says Sash.

"And another," says Tammy.

"Busy boy, aren't we?" says Trixi.

"Trix, listen—"

"Sort him," she says flatly.

They sort me, five of 'em. Trix doesn't get involved. I'm glad of that. She's the worst. But it's still bad. They beat the shit out of me, then stand back, breathing hard. I lie there on the towpath, aching for 'em to go. I can feel the scratches on my face, the blood in my mouth, the bruises all over my body.

Trixi steps forward and looks down.

"Just one last thing," she says.

I brace myself. She's going to kick me in the head. I know it. But I'm wrong.

"Finish it," she says to the girls.

And they crowd around again. I close into a ball. I've got no idea what "finish it" means, but it's going to be bad. They yank my arms back. I wrestle free and close up again. Trixi kicks me in the back.

"Ah!"

"You'll make it worse," she says and then, "Finish it," to the girls.

They force my arms back again, and now I know what they're doing.

"Don't!" I shout. "Please!"

But I can't stop 'em. My clothes are coming off. The jacket first, then the sweater and shirt, then the shoes, socks, trousers. Only the underpants left.

"No." I'm looking up at them. "Please."

They don't even hear me. Off come the underpants, and I'm lying there naked. They stand back and I close up into a ball again. I want to cry. Christ, I want to cry so much.

Don't bloody cry.

They're still standing around me, still looking down.

"Trix, listen—"

"Shut up."

"Trix!"

"I said shut up." She looks down at me with contempt. Enjoyment too. There's no missing that. I'm hugging my knees to my chest, shivering, shaking, fighting tears.

Don't cry. Don't bloody cry.

"Can't see you very well," she says in a low voice.

I say nothing. I don't dare to speak. Trixi glances at her mates, then simply nods. They lean down again.

"No!" I shout.

They force my arms back again, stretch me out, spine against the ground.

Don't cry. Don't bloody cry.

Trixi's looking me over down below.

"Oh, dear," she says. "How disappointing."

Don't cry. Please.

I'm begging myself now. Begging myself not to cry.

She pulls out a knife, flicks it open.

"Don't!" I'm screaming at her. "Don't!"

She laughs. The girls start laughing too. She leans down, plays with the knife.

"Don't what?" she says quietly.

Now the tears come. They flood my eyes so deeply Trixi's face becomes a blur. All I see is the glint of the blade. I feel the scratches on my face sting as the tears run over them.

"Don't," I murmur. "Please don't."

I'm weeping now, weeping like a kid who wants his mummy. Somehow my eyes clear. I see Trixi lean closer. I see the blade approach my face, then move slowly down my body, an inch from the skin.

More tears flood my eyes. I lose sight of her again, then feel my arms and legs released, hear the sound of laughter, and the ripping of fabric. I wipe my eyes with the back of my hand and stare.

The knife's at work but not on me. She's cutting up my clothes. I don't speak, don't move. There's no point. The girls'll do what they want. They've all got knives out now and they're slashing the trousers, shirt, jacket, everything, even the underpants.

They throw the shoes into the canal and chuck the shredded remains of my clothes in after them. Trixi looks down at me and smiles.

"See you around," she says.

And they're gone.

4

YEAH, ALL RIGHT. I know what you're thinking. You're thinking the first lie was when I said I find life easy and the second was when I said I don't need anyone.

But I already admitted I tell lies. You can't pretend I didn't. So there's no point looking at me like that.

Shit, I'm freezing.

Got to find some clothes, got to find somewhere warm. But clothes first. Stand up. Come on. Do it. Christ, I'm swaying on my feet.

Don't just stare at me, Bigeyes. See if you can rescue some of my clothes. No, forget that. They're ruined. Do something else. I don't know. See if you can find something I can wrap around me. A blanket or an old newspaper, whatever.

I know it's a long shot. There's nothing much around here. Just the canal, towpath, bushes, fence.

Walk. Best to walk. Don't go back to the city center. Head for the industrial estate. Someone there might have a spare coat or something.

Walk, walk, walk.

I'm aching all over. Those trolls know how to hurt. And I'm crying again. Wish I could stop but I can't. See that? You were thinking I was just a cocky little tick. Well, I am a cocky little tick but I got feelings too.

Who the hell are those people on the towpath?

Women joggers in matching tracksuits. Three of 'em, talking as they run. Just what I need. Still, at least they won't be scared of me like this. Give 'em a shout.

"Hoy!"

They've seen me.

"Hoy!"

I don't believe it. They're turning back.

"Hoy! Stop!"

They're not stopping. They're putting on speed.

"Hoy! I need help!"

They've gone. Didn't look back once.

Walk on. Shiver, shiver, shiver. God, I hate November. Cold, gray, depressing. Getting dark already. Not a soul in sight since the women ran off.

Hang on. I'm wrong.

Another woman on the towpath but she's no jogger. She's old. White hair, shuffly walk. She shouldn't be out here on her own. Wait a minute. There's something moving in the bushes, something black.

A rottweiler. Whitehair's not so dumb after all. She's spotted me. She's coming on.

Walk. Act confident. No point covering your dingers. She's already seen 'em.

Dog's out of the bushes now, running toward me. She calls out.

"Buffy!"

Dog stops at the sound of her voice. Whitehair comes on. Doesn't look nervous like those joggers did. Stops by the dog, bends down, fits a leash to the collar. I've stopped too. I'm keeping well back from that rottweiler.

Whitehair looks up at me.

"What's happened?" she says.

Sounds Irish. I don't answer. Don't know why. Can't speak.

"You've got blood all around your face," she says. "And scratches everywhere. What's happened to you?"

"Got beaten up."

The woman shakes her head.

"You poor thing."

She starts to take off her coat.

"No," I begin.

But I say no more. I'm dying to wear the coat. I don't care what it looks like. I just want to be warm. I just want to be covered up.

"Put this on," she says.

She walks toward me, holding the coat in one hand and the dog's lead in the other.

"Don't worry about Buffy," she says. "She looks fearsome and if you attacked me, she'd turn nasty. But once she's decided you're a friend, you've got nothing to fear. And she's clearly decided that already."

So it seems. The dog's rubbing herself against me like we're old mates.

I put on the woman's coat.

"Now you're going to get cold," I say.

"Don't worry about me," she says. "Let's get you sorted out. Come on."

She turns and starts to lead me back the way she's come along the towpath.

"Where we going?" I say.

"To my house. It's just over the first bridge. Not very luxurious, I'm afraid, but it's warm and we can ring the police from there."

“No!”

I stop.

She looks around at me.

“Are you in trouble with the police?”

“No, but I don’t like ’em.”

The woman shrugs.

“Well, we’ll talk about what to do later. Let’s just get to the house.”

We walk on in silence.

And you know what, Bigeyes? I’m getting scared again. Don’t know why. I’m not scared of this woman. She’s nice. Must be seventy at least, maybe older. Not too steady on her legs.

But I’m scared, really scared. Like something’s about to happen, only I don’t know what. Might sound crazy, but I trust my feelings, so I’m looking about me as cute as I can.

Trouble is, I’m so cold I can’t think. Coat’s nice and thick and I’ve got all the buttons done up, but the air’s getting in everywhere. The ground’s hard on my bare feet. I’m still stinging all over. My nostrils feel crusted up. Dried blood probably.

I must look a mess.

Whitehair’s cold too. She’s got one of those scruffy cardigans on with buttons up the front and a scraggy old dress down to her shoes, but she’s shivering.

“I’m sorry,” I say.

“What for, dear?”

“Making you shiver.”

She gives me a smile.

“You’re shivering far more than me and I’m not surprised. That coat will only take off the worst of the chill. But we’ll soon have you warm at least. Two more minutes and we're there. See? Just beyond the bridge. That's my house."

And there it is—a little bungalow all by itself on the other side of the canal.

And you know what's weird? I must have passed this place a thousand times and yet now, as I'm hobbling toward it with this white-haired old woman, it's like I've never seen it before.

And I'm still feeling scared.

5

SHE OPENS THE DOOR of the bungalow.

"In you go," she says.

I don't want to go. Don't ask me why. I'm still freezing. The coat's not doing much to help. Here's a house and a friendly old woman, and she's offering me shelter. And I don't want to go in.

"Go on," she says. "You need to get warm."

Still don't move.

She watches me. She's either confused or angry. Can't tell.

"I'll go in," she says, "and I'll leave the door open. You come on in if you want. But if you're not going to come in, can you leave the coat on the step? It's the only decent thing I've got for cold weather."

And in she goes.

Buffy's already charged ahead. God knows where she's disappeared to but I can hear her thumping about in one of the rooms.

Whitehair's halfway down the hall, not even glancing back at me.

It looks like a poky little place, not much furniture and pretty ropy stuff at that. Carpet's knackered too, frayed all over with gaps showing the floorboards underneath.

I'm still standing on the step feeling like a dimp. I just

want Whitehair to turn around. I don't know why. But she's still heading down the hall to the end.

I walk in, close the door behind me. Don't feel better. Warmer but not better. There's a musty smell in this place, like she never cleans it or never lives in it or something. Can't work out what it is.

And I'm getting flashbacks. I've been in a place like this before.

Don't bother asking me where cos I'm not telling you.

Buffy's running back down the hall with an old shoe in her mouth. I suppose this is a present.

"No, thanks."

She drops it at my feet.

"No, thanks."

I'm still feeling strange. I want to turn and run. I don't like these flashbacks.

Whitehair's disappeared into one of the rooms off the hall. I can hear noises like drawers being pulled open. Buffy shoves her head against my bare leg. I push her away. She does it again. She thinks I'm playing.

More flashbacks. I hate this place. I'm really scared. I'm shaking. I can't go outside, not without any clothes, and I can't stay. This place feels all wrong and here's Whitehair coming back. She's carrying a bundle of clothes.

"Now, then," she says, "I don't know if any of these'll fit. Buffy, get out of the way."

She pushes open the door to the room on my left. I go in. A little bedroom. Spare, scrawny, funny smell, just like the rest of the house.

"You can use this room," she says. "Try on the clothes. They used to belong to my grandson."

I'm not even going to tell her she's lying. What's the point? But she is. I got an instinct for lies. I can always tell when someone's zipping me over.

Don't ask me how I know.

But I'm not going to make a fuss. I need some clothes and these are clothes. Crap clothes and probably a bad fit but better than no clothes at all.

She dumps 'em in my arms and closes the door on me.

Turns out they're not bad. Bit baggy and definitely not my style but enough to get me away from here. A knock on the door, then Whitehair's voice.

"Are you decent?"

I open the door.

"How do they feel?" says Whitehair.

She's looking me over, Buffy next to her, thumping her tail on the floor.

"Sweater looks nice and thick," she says. "Bit long but better that than too short. I'll get you a belt and those trousers will feel better. We'll sort out some shoes for you later. Now then—we must ring your parents at once."

And this silence falls between us.

Buffy picks it up and stops banging her tail against the floor. Whitehair's watching me closely. First time I've noticed she's got green eyes. They're not unfriendly but I've stopped trusting her.

"Why don't you trust me?" she says.

She's speaking my thoughts for me now. I don't answer. She gives me this smile. Don't trust that either.

"Is it because you don't trust anyone?" she says.

"What are you, a shrink?"

She doesn't answer that, just shrugs.

"Where do you live?" she says eventually. "I can order a taxi to get you home. I'll pay for it."

I'm not telling her anything. It's none of her business. And I'm not telling you anything either, Bigeyes, so don't keep looking at me.

I'm getting more uneasy by the minute. Whitehair's too close.

"Move back." I glare at her. "Move back."

She stays where she is, just watches.

"My name's Mary," she says.

Her voice has changed. It's really low, like she doesn't want me to hear it, like I've got to stay this close to her if I'm going to hear it. I take a step back.

She doesn't move, just goes on watching, then speaks again, same low voice.

"I'm from Ireland. Small village down in the south."

Like I give two bells where she comes from. She can come from the North Pole for all I care. She's not what she pretends to be. I know it.

"Do you want to tell me your name?" she says.

I can see her green eyes moving over me. What's she looking at? She should keep her eyes on my face.

"I'm watching your hands," she says suddenly. "I can see I'm making you nervous. But you're making me nervous now. So I'm watching your hands."

"What for?"

"In case you attack me."

"Keep your distance and I won't."

Another big silence. We're both staring at each other. I glance at Buffy. She's watching me too, and she's changed.

We're not friends now. She's picked up I might be trouble. She'll rip me apart if I go for Mary.

"What are you frightened of?" says the old woman.

"Not you."

"What are you frightened of?"

I don't answer. I'm watching Buffy. She's all tensed up, like she's going to jump or snap.

"Buffy," says Mary. "Easy, easy."

Her voice is like a murmur now. The dog relaxes. Mary's eyes look suddenly soft. Soft and green. She looks back at me.

"Come and have some tea," she says.

6

THE KITCHEN. Is this dronky or what? Look at that stove. Something from the Dark Ages. Not much in the way of lighting either. Mary's burning a candle, one of those fat, scented ones. She's got it on a saucer on the table.

"Sit down," she says.

Buffy's close by. Looks confused. Doesn't know whether to lick my hand or bite it off.

I sit down at the table. Candle's flickering. Mary's lighting another one over on the shelf. She sits down, other side of the table. I can see she's keeping her distance.

Fine by me. She looks at me. I look back.

"Yeah?"

"Easy," she says.

I feel Buffy's nose against my hand. Stroke her. She licks my palm. Mary smiles.

"She trusts you again. That's good. Shame you don't feel able to trust us in return."

"I trust Buffy."

"Why don't you trust me?"

I shrug. The candle on the table goes out.

Mary lights it again.

"I don't know anything about you," she says. "Except you've been beaten up and stripped of your clothes. And I want to help. That's it. Nothing more. I have no wish to keep you here. There's nothing to stop you from running out the front door if you want to. Except perhaps some shoes. Hold on."

She stands up.

"I'll go and find the last few things you'll need and then you'll have no reason to stay if you don't want to."

Her face has changed. It's toughened. She walks out, Buffy following, but she's soon back. She's holding some shoes and an old coat.

"Here you are," she says. She drops 'em in the doorway. "Oh, and I promised a belt."

Again she's gone and again soon back. She drops a long black belt on the pile, followed by a brown envelope.

"That's a little money in case it's useful. I don't need to be paid back. Just keep it."

Not sure what to say or feel. She sits down again at the table.

"Thanks," I manage.

She gives me a brief smile, then leans toward the candle. I can see her face flickering under the moving flame.

"Is there anybody you want me to ring to say where you are?" she says.

"How are you going to ring anyone when you haven't got a phone in the house?"

"How do you know I haven't got a phone in the house?"

"I've seen."

"Not all the rooms. You haven't been in all the rooms."

"I glanced in the doors."

"All of them?"

"Yeah."

"I didn't see you do that."

"No reason why you should. I'm good at keeping an eye open. Seeing stuff."

I have to be, Bigeyes, know what I mean? The porkers would have banged me up loads of times otherwise.

She's watching me over the flame.

"Real little survivor, aren't you?" she says.

Buffy takes a step back from me. I can feel the atmosphere change. I'm dangerous again, and there's no question whose side Buffy's on.

I look back at Mary.

"I checked in the rooms on my way here. You went on ahead and left me to follow. So I glanced through the doors."

"And you saw no phone?"

"Yeah."

"What else did you see?"

"Stuff that doesn't look like it belongs to an old woman."

"Like what?"

"Like a train set."

"It's my grandson's."

"You haven't got a grandson."

"How do you know?"

"I just do. I can tell when someone's zipping me over."

"What does that mean?"

"Work it out for yourself."

She moves back from the flame but the light goes on dancing over her face. She frowns suddenly.

"You're very sharp. And you're right about the phone. There isn't a phone in the house. But you don't know I haven't got a mobile."

"Yes, I do."

"You can't. You haven't looked in my bag." She gives a start. "Have you?"

I wait, deliberately, then, "No, I haven't been through your bag. I don't need to. I just know you haven't got a mobile."

"Instinct? Is that it? Or are you psychic?"

There's a hard tone in her voice now.

"Call it what you like," I say.

She looks down at the flame. I can smell the scent from both candles. One's lemon, the other's lavender. She speaks again.

"Why would I offer to ring someone on your behalf if I didn't think I could do so?"

I don't answer. I'm looking at Buffy. She's all tensed up like she's going to snap at me any moment. I've got to get out of here. Whatever it is about this old girl, there's something not right. She's helped me out of a spot and she's probably harmless but I don't trust her. And anyway, I've got places to go. I can't stay here.

"I was going to go out to the phone booth," she says. "There's one just down by the towpath."

"I know."

"I was going to use that."

"It's been vandalized."

"Oh."

She looks surprised and for the first time I almost believe her. But I've still got to go. Something's all wrong here. Buffy's quivering, her eyes fixed on me. Mary's watching too.

I stand up.

"Got to go."

"Okay."

"Thanks for the clothes."

"It's okay. Try the other things on."

I put on the belt, shoes, coat.

"Do they fit?" she says.

"They're okay."

I pick up the envelope, glance inside. Hundred quid.

"Very generous."

"It's no problem."

"I don't need it."

"You can't use a hundred pounds?"

"I can use it but I don't need it."

"You've got plenty of money?"

"I got to go."

"All right."

I drop the envelope on the table. Buffy bares her teeth.

"Easy," says Mary.

It takes me a moment to realize she's not talking to the dog.

"What did you think I was going to do?" I say.

"I don't know." The old woman's watching me closely. "That's why I'm scared of you."

I look down, look up.

"I don't want you to be scared of me."

She says nothing. I move toward the door, stop. There's that feeling again. Something's still wrong, something else. Can't work out what it is. But Buffy's restless again and this time it's not cos of me.

"What is it?" says Mary.

I don't answer. I'm listening. All I can hear is the hiss of the candle on the shelf as the wax runs down. Otherwise silence, in the house, around the house. But it's still not right. I've felt this before, many times, and I'm never wrong.

"There's someone near the house," I say.

"What makes you say that?" says Mary.

Before I can answer, the kitchen window shatters and a brick comes flying through.

I see two figures standing outside.

7

7 Men. Hard-looking gobbos. Never seen 'em before.

Buffy's barking her head off. Mary's on her feet, pushing me into the hall. She doesn't need to. I want to wig it out of here quick as blink.

"Run!" she says.

I run for the front door. Yeah, yeah, I know what you're thinking. I ought to stick it out with her. Bollocks. I'm racing down the hall. Another crash from the kitchen window, then a shadow in the front door.

Stop, think, but there's no time.

The glass in the front door smashes and there's a third gobbo looking in. Big grunt of a guy. I hear Mary's voice behind me.

"The window! Main bedroom! Climb out and run!"

I'm already racing past her. Another crash from the kitchen, more shattering glass, then a bang on the front door. The grunt's got something big pounding against it.

Buffy's charging about, still barking. Voices from the kitchen, heavy voices. The gobbos are climbing through the window. Here's the main bedroom.

Stop at the door, look back.

Mary's just standing in the hall. She hasn't moved. Buffy's stopped too, right beside her, stopped barking even, like they're waiting, just waiting for what's coming. She shouts at me suddenly.

"Run!"

I run through the main bedroom, open the window. No figures on the outside, just the dronky back garden of the bungalow and beyond that the canal. I climb out, tumble onto the hard ground, jump up and run toward the fence.

Voices inside the house, men's voices shouting, roaring. No sound of Mary, just Buffy barking again. A crash from the other end of the house. The grunt's almost smashed in the front door.

Stop, think, breathe.

I know, I know. Don't keep telling me, okay?

I creep back to the house, slow, slow. Don't ask me what I'm going to do cos I haven't got a clue. Probably no use anyway. What can I do against those gobbos?

But I can't leave the old girl. I know she was lying to me but she did rescue me. She did give me the clothes. I'm trembling. Why's it gone so quiet? Even Buffy's gone quiet. No voices, no banging and crashing, nothing.

I'm close to the window now, right by it. Still silence.

Then the gunshot.

I freeze. I'm clutching the window, shaking. Silence again, dead silence. Inside, outside, like the world's gone still.

Bang!

A second gunshot.

And I'm gone. Over the lawn, over the fence, out to the road, off toward the industrial estate. Don't try and stop me. Waste of time yakking in my head. I don't care what's right or wrong. Mary's dead. That's all I know. Buffy too, probably.

I'm wigging it out of here.

Don't look back, don't stop. I hate this road. Empty bloody thing, craggy fence, scrawny fields either side. Nowhere to hide if those gobbos come out. They'll see me straightaway. They know there's a witness. They saw me inside the house.

But there's no other way out of here. I'm not going back along the canal. That's even more exposed. If I can just get to the industrial buildings, I'll be all right for a bit.

Hundred yards, fifty, twenty. I'm panting but I'm nearly there.

GJB Electronics UK. Am I pleased to see you? Around the side of the building, over the parking lot, down to the Dumpsters, through them and on to the low wall. Over and on to the next site. Down the side of the tire depot, past the welder's, on around the back of the builder's yard.

Stop, lean against the wall, breathe, think.

Can't think. Keep seeing pictures of Mary. I was hard on her. She was lying but she was helping me. She offered me money. She'd have let me take it. Those women joggers wigged it but Mary stopped and helped me.

Don't look at me like that. I feel bad enough already. I don't need you dumping guilt on me as well.

Mary. I keep seeing those eyes, keep seeing those candles glowing on her face.

Get up. Come on, get up.

I get up. Don't feel better but I'm on my feet and I know what I'm going to do. I can't do anything for Mary but I might be able to shunt those gobbos.

Think. Come on, think. Get your brain working again.

Over the builder's yard, out the other side. That's better. Moving's good, thinking's good. Over the fence, down to the end of the estate. Getting dark now. City's all bright but it's dark around here. Those lights might as well come from Mars.

There's the phone. I'm just praying no one's smashed it up. Looks okay. Check it out. Dial tone's fine. Breathe, think, calm down. Another breath. I hate talking to porkers. Another breath. Right, do it.

Nine . . . one . . . one . . .

Quick answer. Woman's voice, nice voice, kind of warm, kind of friendly. Sort of person you'd want to talk to. Only I can't do it. Don't look at me like that. I just can't do it, okay? She's talking again, asking me which service I want.

I put the phone down. I put the bloody phone down.

Got to think, got to be alone, got to be somewhere safe. Just as well I know the very place. But it means I've got to let you in on a secret.

8

NOW LISTEN, COS I'm going to tell you something nobody knows and I'm not sure I can trust you. No, I'll put that another way. I DON'T trust you. All right? I don't trust you one little bit.

Why should I? I don't even know you. I've told you my favorite name but that's all. You're just hanging around. You maybe thought I was a bit spitty for not trusting Mary. I wasn't being spitty. If you'd seen what I've seen in fourteen years, you'd learn not to trust. And you wouldn't want to spend time talking on the phone to porkers either.

How do I know you're not going to shunt me? Well, I'll take a chance on you. I need some company tonight. But you keep what I tell you to yourself, okay? Right, here's the thing.

Most kids like me don't last. They slap it for a bit, sleeping rough, getting cold, then before they know it, they're starving, shivering, drugged out. If they're not banged up by the porkers, then some other gobbos are using 'em, know what I mean?

Or they're dead.

Or they're back home with Mummy.

None of that applies to me. Why? I told you before—I'm different. I don't get many nights when I have to slap it. Five nights out of seven, I'm snugged out and nobody owns me. Cos nobody knows I'm there.

How do I do it? Simple. Simple and tricky at the same time.

First you got to know the city. This girl takes some knowing and she's fickle. She changes all the time. Sometimes she's a queen, sometimes she's a bit of a dingo. And she's big, big, big.

That can be good or it can be scary. Depends on her mood. She can love you one minute, bite your head off the next. I don't always like her. But I do respect her and I'll tell you this—I know her.

I know her like nobody in the world knows her. I told you earlier that I see things no one else can. Well, sometimes it's like I see everything that happens.

You smirking at me?

Don't shake your head. I can see you smirking at me. Well, stop, cos I'm telling the truth. I see stuff and that's cos I know the city, and cos I watch. It starts with watching. You got to take your time and see how things work.

Took me years to learn it. When I was little—I mean dead little and those ticks still had their hands on me—I couldn't manage it. I couldn't move cos of them and even when I broke free, I was spinning like a top.

But I told you—I see things, and I learn quick. And the first thing I learned was how to watch. I watched the city. I watched her day and night, just like I do now. You got to do it all the time so you don't miss anything. It's when you're not watching that you get caught.

So you stay one step ahead, always one step ahead.

First thing I noticed when I started watching the city—really watching, I mean—was how many people don't live in their homes. Yeah, I know—most people do. I'm not interested in them. It's the ones who don't that matter. You got to be patient to find out who they are.

But it's worth it. If you watch long enough, you find there's snug empty homes all over the city. Most nights I'm spoiled for choice. Sometimes, like I say, there's nowhere and I have to slap it like any other duff.

But it's rare. Tonight I could name three places to snug out. So we'll take the best.

Come with me and I'll show you a bit of my world. Just a bit, mind. Don't get any ideas. But I need to talk. I need to get my mind straight. I'm messed up. First the stuff with Trixi, then Mary and that crazy dog. So you can stick around with me a bit longer.

But don't lag behind. I can't talk if you're behind me. Right, see that light over there? Other side of the wall? It's a little burger kiosk. Guy called Abdel runs it with his son. Look to the right. Entrance to the park. We're going that way.

Not into the city. We'll keep away from that. We're heading for the outskirts.

Walk, walk, walk.

Walking helps, helps you think, and when you don't want to think, it helps that too. Sometimes I walk thirty miles in a day, sometimes more.

Walk to think, walk to forget. Doesn't always work but it can help.

Here's the wall. No point going the long way around. Climb over, drop down, check around. Gangs use this park sometimes. Trixi and those other trolls hang about here, and all kinds of other nebs. So keep your eyes open.

Walk, walk. Into the park, through the trees, over the soccer field.

Watch. Keep watching. That's how you stay alive. I know Trixi got me earlier but that should be a warning to you. If I can get caught, anyone can.

So watch. Trixi's the least of your worries around here.

Walk on, leave the soccer field, through the other gate, out of the park. See the lights to the left? City's waking up. Different energy at night. Can you feel it? She's beautiful when you're on the outside looking in. I'm feeling better for walking.

Not right though. Not right at all. Keep seeing Mary's face.

I need to snug out. I need it badly. But it's not far now.

Past the allotments, past the gas station. More allotments. Houses thinning out, see? Keep to the side of the road. Keep close to the front gardens.

Walk small. We can't use this place if anyone sees us. We'll have to use one of the other snugs. But we should be all right. They're mostly old nebs living around here and the curtains are drawn across. Just a few more yards and . . .

Welcome to the snug.

9

Now do exactly what I do. Keep your eyes open and above all keep quiet. If you give me away, we're finished. You and me, I mean. Mess up one of my snugs and we part company.

Right, keep low. Every snug's different but the rules are the same. You go in unseen, you stay in unseen, you come out unseen, and nobody—NOBODY—ever knows you've been in there. Least of all the owners. So watch, copy and learn.

First thing with this snug, we go around the back. It's an old couple owns this house. Dotty old nebs. She's sixty-one, he's seventy-two. I watched 'em for a year or more before I decided to use their place. Like I told you, you got to keep watching. I'm watching loads of places and loads of people all the time. That's how I know what's going on.

The best people are the ones who aren't like me. Where I notice everything, they notice nothing. Take the nebs who live here. I know their names, their dates of birth, their hobbies, their histories. I know the names and addresses of their families and friends, the guy they use to do their plumbing, the kind of food they like.

What do they know about me?

Nothing. They don't even know I exist. And they don't know that ten or more times in the last six months I've been snugging out in their house.

How do I find out all this stuff about them? Easy. From the

things they leave around the place. It's all there for you and they never know you know, as long as you're careful and you make sure everything—EVERYTHING—is exactly as it was when you leave as when you went in.

Touch stuff, yeah, but put it back exactly as it was.

Like I say, the best snugs to use are the ones owned by people who don't notice stuff. I could probably move things in this house and the dear old nebs wouldn't notice when they got back.

But I don't take that risk. I'm careful. I'm good at what I do. That's why I'm still here. That's why I'm in control.

Okay, around the back. See that little shed? Bottom of the garden? They don't use it for much. Couple of spades and a lawn mower. Bits and bobs. Come around the back of it and I'll show you something.

See that old stone? Lift it up.

Presto! Back-door key to the house. Well, copy of the key. These nebs are a sweet pair. When they're in the house, they leave the back door unlocked and the key still in the lock. Then they sit in the front room and watch TV.

When they go away every weekend to stay with their son and his family, they lock the back door and put the key in the kitchen drawer. By the time I'd worked out where they were going every Friday, I'd got a copy made of the key.

Lovely old couple. Regular as clockwork in everything. Taxi picks 'em up at ten in the morning every Friday. Same cab company, usually same guy. He gets out and puts their cases in the trunk.

The old girl says, "How are you?" and they have a little natter while the old boy struggles into the cab. Anyone with a bit of patience and a decent pair of ears can find out that they're off to the station to go and stay with their boy and they won't be coming back till Sunday.

If the driver was a crook, there'd be trouble, not just for the old nebs but for me. But he's not, so I guess we're all lucky. Anyway, come on in but keep to the right. You got to stay out of the sight line from next door. Keep to this side of the path and they can't see you. And don't make a sound or knock anything.

Let's go.

Key in the back door. See? Turns cute. Open the door, slow. It used to squeak a bit but I put some oil on the hinges last time I snugged out here. Close the door. Lock it. Take the key out.

Keep still, listen. Make sure everything's okay. We should be all right. With some of the snugs you need to ring to make sure the nebs have gone. Can't do that here. You're exposed on the front doorstep and the neighbors can see you.

But it's okay. I know the signs. No key in the back door. See? It's in the kitchen drawer like I told you. Curtains in the front room drawn back. No lights on in the house. All quiet. They're not here.

But we'll give each room an eyeball. Always do that. Check everything. Make sure we're safe.

Right, shoes off. Park 'em out of sight behind the tumble dryer. Walk slow. Rule one—never move fast in the darkness. Rule two—don't switch anything on, especially the lights, not unless I say it's all right.

Sometimes it's okay. All the snugs are different. Some of 'em you can switch lights on, listen to the radio, watch TV, other stuff. Sometimes you can have a bath or a shower, cook a meal, whatever. As long as you clean up afterward so it's exactly like it was before, nobody ever knows.

Here you can't do too much. All the rooms except one have got a window and any nebs outside'll see the light easy. Same thing with noise. You got to be really careful here. Next door'll hear if you play something too loud.

But I don't come here for that anyway. Not this snug. I mean, we'll put the radio on later really low so I can hear if there's any news about Mary. But that's the only thing I want the radio for. Like I say, I don't come to this snug for the radio or the TV.

I come here to read.

Cos these old nebs are bung-crazy about books.

I didn't use to like 'em but I really got into 'em now. Sometimes, when I'm off my head, it's books that calm me down. Not always. When I'm getting flashbacks, nothing can sort me. But I still like books and these two have got hundreds.

Come on. We need to check out downstairs.

Nice and quiet, nice and dark. I love the darkness. You can wrap up in it. It's like a warm bed, and there's an even warmer bed waiting for me upstairs.

All clear down here. See all the books? When's the last time you saw that many in one place? They can't possibly read 'em all.

Back down the hall. Mind the pictures. Don't knock 'em off-line.

Up the stairs. Walk quiet, just in case.

Stop on the landing, look around.

More books, see? Shelves groaning. Books, books, books.

Same in all the upstairs rooms. They've even got books in the bathroom. Look at this one. I tried it last time I came here.

Superman and the Will to Power.

I thought it'd be comics but there's no pictures at all, just a load of stuff about a gobbo called Nietzsche. Never mind, try this one.

Treasure Island.

Now that's what I call a story. I've read it six times, maybe more. Every time I come here, I read a whole book. Nonstop, every word. I read fast. Book a night, no problem. Other snugs have got books too and sometimes I don't have to read in the dark.

But it doesn't make any difference.

As long as I can see the words, I'm all right.

Only I didn't finish *Treasure Island* last time I came here. I was tired. I had to sleep. I just got to the bit where Jim Hawkins is hiding in the apple barrel and listening to the pirates plotting, and then Long John Silver says, "Fetch me an apple" to one of his mates, and at that moment . . .

Shh!

Don't make a sound, Bigeyes.

There's someone by the back door.

10

KEEP STILL. Stay behind me on the landing. Let me peep around the side of the stairway.

Nobody. I can see all the way down to the back door. But somebody's out there. Don't ask me how I know.

Shh!

Footsteps in the garden, a shadow coming toward the door. Stops. I can see him now. It's the grunt I saw outside Mary's front door. Ugly-looking gobbo. I can see him better from up here than when I was close to him at Mary's. He can't see me on the landing, not with this shadow.

But he's not looking anyway. He's staring at the door. He's bending down, fiddling with something. Shit, he's picking the lock.

Quick—and quiet!

Down the landing to the end, open the little door, up the other stairway. Freeze! A rattling noise. Can you hear it? Well, I can. He's not in yet but he soon will be. Top of the stairway, push open the door.

Lumber room.

Nothing else for it. Hide in one of those big cardboard boxes. Not the tea chests. Too obvious. Try the box in the corner.

Can't hear anything downstairs.

That's even more dangerous. We're top of the house now.

We wouldn't hear much down there. He might be in, he might not.

Listen.

Silence. Deep silence.

I just know he's in.

We got to be silent too. And not a sound getting into that box.

Climb in. Slow, slow, ease in. Now then—pull the lids down.

Don't breathe.

Just wait and listen.

Not a sound downstairs, not a breath, not a whisper. But he's in. I know it. He's in and he's looking for me. There's no way this is coincidence. I see the grunt through Mary's front door. He sees me. Him and the gobbos break in and shoot Mary. See me running away.

A witness.

Grunt sees which way I go and follows. Probably got his two mates with him in the street. I must have missed 'em on the way here.

We're in the grime, Bigeyes.

I'm telling you. We're in the grime.

Footsteps. Hear that? Down on the landing.

They've stopped. No, they're starting again. He's taking his time, getting his bearings, checking every room.

No sign of a light. Not using a flashlight, not yet anyway. He can use one in this room. The only room in the house with no window. The place I come to read. Only now it's the place I'm going to get killed.

Silence again. What's he doing now? I can't work out

where he is. I thought I had him underneath me in the spare bedroom. Now I'm not so sure.

Footsteps again. He's in the main bedroom, not moving so quiet now that he's worked out the owners aren't here. He knows he's either alone in the house or it's just him and me.

Either way he's laughing.

He's more confident now. I can tell from the sound.

He's almost relaxed.

Click!

He's found the door to the stairway up to this room. He's opening it.

Silence.

Can't hear him but I can feel him now. Bottom of the stairway, looking up to the top. I just know he's looking up. He's looking up and listening out for some clue that I'm here. In a moment he'll make his way up, and as soon as he sees there's no window in the lumber room, he'll put the light on, or switch a flashlight on.

And I'm finished.

Footsteps on the stairway.

Slow, slow, quite heavy now, but he's happy. If no one's up here, no one'll hear 'em. If I'm up here, he wants me to hear 'em. He wants me to be scared.

They stop.

Top of the stairway. Heavy breathing, wheezing. Door pushes open. Two more steps, three, stop.

Grunt's in the room.

Crouch down, keep low, don't make a sound. Can't see a thing, just the side of the cardboard box, all bleary with darkness. I'm quivering. There's no way out of this.

Bing!

Light goes on.

Knew he'd do that. Silence again. He's looking around, just standing there. I can picture his grunty head moving. Heavy breathing again. He's worn himself out climbing two lots of stairs but he's still too dangerous to take on. If I can wriggle past him, I might be able to wig it, but if he grabs me, I'm done.

Steps again. He's walking this way.

Stops. Sound of rummaging. He's poking in the tea chest. Growling noise, a sniffle, a sneeze, sound of wiping. Probably his sleeve against his nose. More rummaging in the tea chest.

Stops.

Footsteps again, closer. More rummaging. He's trying some of the other cardboard boxes. Maybe this is the time to run. While he's fiddling with the other boxes, I might be able to squeeze past him and down the stairs.

Too late. The rummaging's stopped and he's moving again.

He's by the box. My box. He's breathing hard. Another sneeze, a big globby sneeze. Something grabs hold of my box, starts to fiddle with the lids, then—

A mobile rings.

He stops. I'm trembling inside the box. The lids are still in place but he's moved them just enough for me to peer up through the gap and see the side of his face. He's got a mobile clapped to his ear.

"Yeah, mate?"

He's got a voice like a sinking ship.

A pause, then he goes on.

"He's not here. Any sign of him where you are?"

Another pause.

"All right," he says. "Meet you there."

He hangs up.

I want to twist my face away. The moment he looks down, he'll see my eyes watching him through the gap between the lids of the box. But he doesn't look down. He's walking back to the door. Another resounding sneeze, then the light goes off, and step, step, step down to the landing.

I don't hear the back door go, just the tramp of his feet around the side of the house and out into the street.

And then they're gone.

11

I'M OUT OF THE BOX, down the stairs, into the main bedroom, over to the window.

There he goes down the street, not looking back, not looking at the other houses. He's talking on his mobile again. I watch him go, watch him all the way down the street. No sign of the other two, no sign of anyone. That's why I used to like this street. There's never anybody around.

I don't feel so safe here now.

Slump down. Got to think, got to really think. They're looking for me, no question. They think I saw 'em kill Mary or whatever. Unless . . .

No, it can't be that. It can't be anything to do with that. Surely . . .

Thing is, Bigeyes, something I haven't told you—there's other people looking for me. Never mind why. All you need to know is that I got enemies. And it's big stuff, okay? Serious grime. And it goes back a long way.

Trouble is, the people I'm really scared of won't come themselves. They'll send other people. They might have sent these gobbos.

So that grunt and his two mates, they could be after me cos they think I saw 'em stick the clapper on Mary. Or they could be from the other lot, and that would be even worse. It'd mean they've tracked me to the city.

I didn't think they could do that. I didn't think anyone

could do that. I thought I could just come here and play dead.

It's been working for the last three years. I've been under the radar all this time. No one in the city knows me. Not really. I mean, some people think they know me.

Trixi thinks she knows me cos she caught me working one of her streets last year, and there are others who think they know me. You still got to deal with people, even when you're playing dead. You got to buy food and do stuff.

But I'm still a ghost. I sleep where I want. I go where I want. I call myself what I want. Even the porkers haven't touched me since I came to the city. They've never even met me. I'll be on their records from the old days but they haven't seen me since I came here. And that's how I want it.

I'm starting to feel scared. And I'm still choked up about Mary. Keep seeing pictures of her lying dead. But I can't stay slumped here.

Got to go through the ritual. Clean up, eat, drink, sleep. Stay well, stay alive.

Come on, stop shaking. Stand up, move. Out of the bedroom, through the darkness, into the bathroom. What did I tell you, Bigeyes? Books in here as well. Don't ask me what kind of plant that is. I haven't got a clue and I don't give two bells anyway.

Run the tap.

Water feels good. Face still stings from where those trolls got me but I don't care. Water's cool. I'd like to use the shower but I'm too tired and I still feel a bit vulnerable here. I didn't use to feel that way, but seeing the grunt in one of my snugs has fizzed me out.

Dry my face, mop up all around with toilet paper, flush down the toilet. No traces. Nothing to show I've been here.

I'm still trembling, Bigeyes. Can't stop. Why can't I stop?

Find a book. That'll help. Might not stop it but it can't do any harm. Here's one. An old favorite.

Wind in the Willows.

I'll read that later. But eat first. Out of the bathroom, down the stairs. Keep away from the walls, Bigeyes. I told you before. You mustn't knock any of the pictures off-line. That one's already off-line. Grunt must have barged it as he went past. It wasn't me.

Straighten it, move on down the stairs.

He's left the back door unlocked.

Lock it again, move to the kitchen. Should be plenty of food here. That's why I like this place. They're not organized, these nebs. Too many books and too much food. Open that cupboard.

See?

Baked bean cans all over the place. How can two people possibly need that many baked beans? And look at all these other cans. God knows what they've got in here. Check out the bread basket.

Loads.

Okay, can of baked beans, can of sweet corn, can of button mushrooms, three slices of toast. Grill on, toast under. Saucepans on the rings. Power on.

Now this is where you got to be careful. No lights on but a little glow from the rings on the cooker. If the grunt was out in the garden now, he'd notice. We should be okay cos we're not on the sight line from next door, but keep a watch.

And here's the other risky bit.

I'm turning on the radio, just low. But I got to hear if there's any news about Mary. Someone might have found her body.

"The headlines today. The prime minister has come under fire in the House of Commons over the government's plans to increase . . ."

But there's nothing. Political stuff, new cancer drug, global warming, some actor's died. Nothing about Mary. Turn the toast, stir the food, switch off the radio.

Don't want to hear any more.

I'm choked up. What's happened to her? I keep thinking about her lying dead on the floor. I should have had the guts, should have phoned the porkers. I still could. There's a phone here.

But I know I won't.

Eat. Come on, got to eat. Plate, knife, fork. Butter the toast, scoop on the food. Smells good. Just wish I was going to enjoy it. But I can't. I'm still thinking about Mary.

Can't eat this stuff, can't eat any of it, can't eat, can't think.

Tip the food away, push it right down inside the trash, cover it over. Wash up, dry up, put everything away just as it was. Go and sleep. Tomorrow'll be better. I know what I've got to do tomorrow. But sleep first. Got to blank this all out.

Up the stairs, hold the book tight, don't let it go.

Wind in the Willows.

You know the bit I'm going to read? The bit where Ratty and Mole are in the snow and Mole suddenly smells his old home, and they go back and find it again. I'm going to read that bit before I fall asleep.

But I'm not going up to the lumber room.

I need to lie down. I need to be warm. I can read in the dark. I don't even need to see the words, not with this book. I know them anyway.

Top of the stairs, spare bedroom. This is where I always sleep. I roll up in that old duvet. Jump on the bed, wrap the duvet around. It's an old friend. I recognize the smell. Feels good, feels warm and dark.

Open the book.

I can see the words better than I thought. Flick through. Here's the chapter. *Dulce Domum.* It's Latin, I found out. Don't know what it means. But this is the chapter where Mole finds his old home. He follows the scent and then dives down into the ground and finds his little house.

This is where you leave me, Bigeyes.

I want to be by myself now. Just me and little Mole. So get lost.

I'll see you in the morning.

12

WAKE UP. It's six o'clock.

Time to move. Got to sort this thing with Mary. And we got to get out of here before anyone sees us. Should be okay. Like I told you, they're mostly old nebs around here and it's a sleepy place. But you can't be too careful.

Check the bedroom. Tidy up. Check again.

Book back on the shelf, same place. Check around. No marks, nothing on the floor. Bathroom. Wash, dry, tidy up. Check around. Down the stairs. Not bothering with breakfast. Still can't eat, worrying too much about Mary. Got to find out what happened.

Kitchen. Check around, shoes from behind the tumble dryer. Put 'em on. Check out the garden. All clear, all quiet. Blackbird on the fence, robin on the shed. Cold sky.

No nebs in sight.

Key in the door, open slowly, listen. Hum of traffic beyond the estate, nothing else. Push open the door, peer out. All clear. Step out, lock the door, over to the shed, key under the stone. Back down the path and around the side of the house.

Check the street. Nice and quiet. Looks almost quaint.

Why don't I feel so good?

Come on, Bigeyes. We got to move.

Down the street, past the allotments, away. On to Barton Avenue, right at the junction. Keep close, Bigeyes, don't lag.

Over the railway bridge, across the field, down the alley, through the park.

All quiet, but you still got to watch. You never stop watching. Mostly it's dog walkers this time of day but there's still danger. You still got to be careful. Like I told you—I got people after me. I got to see 'em before they see me, you understand?

Keep moving. Don't slow down.

Outskirts of the city. She's waking up now. She's still a bit sleepy but she's stretching her arms and yawning. Cars, buses, cyclists. Lots of nebs out already. Students, suits, kids, shopkeepers opening up. Couple of porkers, traffic warden.

All muffins so far. Nobody dangerous. But you don't usually see the dangerous ones. That's why you watch, Bigeyes. That's why you never stop watching.

Left here and down the slip road, through the underpass, left again. We're coming to the bungalow from the other side. Slow down a bit now.

Don't want to show ourselves.

There's the canal. See it? Over to the left. Keep back a bit. Use the parked cars to hide behind. Slowly forward. Check around. Keep checking around. I don't feel right about this place. Those gobbos could be still close. They know I've been here once. They might be watching in case I come back.

Can't see 'em. Can't see anyone.

There's the road up to the industrial estate. There's the bungalow. Looks quiet enough. No porkers outside. No police cars. Nobody at all. Couple of joggers on the canal. Lanky guy and a woman. But that's about it.

Check around. Move closer to the bungalow. Get ready to run any moment. Don't like these parked cars now. They're hiding me but they might be hiding other people.

Move on, slow, slow.

Still nobody around. Lorry moving up the road toward the industrial estate. Couple of cars and a mail truck. Soon gone. Stop by the last parked car. Keep close to it, keep low, peer over the road.

The bungalow looks just like it did. Front door closed but the glass panel smashed in. None of the windows open as far as I can see. Wait a moment. . . .

Front door's not closed. I thought it was but it's ajar. I'm sure it's ajar.

Need to get closer to be certain.

Check around. Check left, right, behind.

Over the road, stop at the front gate. Check again. Through the gate and up to the front door.

I was right. It's ajar. The grunt pounded it so hard he broke it open.

Check through. I can see good. Nobody in the hall, just glass and splinters over the carpet.

Move back. It's too risky to go in. I just know it. Around the side of the house, soft, really soft. Don't make a sound. First window. Keep to the side, edge close, peep around. The bedroom I got changed in. Nobody in there.

Next window. Bathroom. Misted glass. Next window.

Curtains drawn across.

Listen.

Not a sound inside but something's wrong about this room. Don't ask me how I know. Around the other side of the bungalow. Kitchen windows smashed in. I'm standing where the two gobbos were standing last night.

Look through.

Nothing there. Just glass all over the floor. Candle's still on the table. It's burned right down.

No sign of Mary or the porkers or anybody. But I'm thinking about that bedroom. I don't like this, Bigeyes. I'm telling you, I don't like this. I want to run. But I feel I owe Mary something. She could be lying in there undiscovered.

She might even be still alive.

Around to the front door. I'm trembling again. I hate this. Calm down. Keep your wits about you. Move quiet. Stop by the door. Listen hard, look through again. Nobody. Push open the door, slowly. Leave it wide open. May have to run like blood.

Creep in. Splinters of glass underfoot. Step over them. Check around. Still nobody. No movement, no shadow, no breathing. But danger. I can feel it.

Whirl around.

Doorway's still clear. I can see right out to the street.

Turn back. Creep down the hall. Stop by the kitchen. Check right. Nobody there. Over to the main bedroom.

Door's closed.

Stop, listen.

Not a sound. Check back down the hall. Still empty, still quiet. Ear to the bedroom door. Nothing, just the sound of my own breathing.

Turn the doorknob. Get ready to run.

No reaction to the sound, no shout from inside the room. But that means nothing. I push open the door, stand back.

"Shit!"

She's lying on the floor by the side of the bed, staring toward the ceiling, an upturned chair close by. But it's not Mary.

It's Trixi.

13

I WANT TO RUN FOR it but my legs take me straight in. I kneel down.

"Trix!"

She's not breathing. Her eyes are glazed. There's a bruise on her head the size of a scream.

"Trix!"

A voice, but not from her.

"I'm afraid she's beyond your help."

I whip around, jump up.

There's a guy standing behind the door, one of the gobbos I saw peering through the kitchen window last night. He's been in the room all the time. And there's a third figure.

One of the trolls from Trixi's gang. Don't know her name. She's slumped in the far corner. Her eyes are glazed too, but she's not dead. She's choked out with fear.

The gobbo glances at her.

"Lost her voice, poor thing. They're all the same, these kids. Think they're tough because they're part of a gang and the first sign of violence they fall apart." He bellows at her, "Don't you!"

She doesn't answer, just shivers. She's white. She's all closed up. I'll get no help from her. The gobbo closes the door, looks over at me.

"I was hoping you might come back."

I look around. Got to be something I can do.

"There's nothing," says the man, watching me. "Nothing you can do."

"What do you want?"

"You, my friend. I thought that was obvious."

"What for?"

"Because of who you are."

"And who am I?"

"Oh, we're clever, are we? Quick-witted? I was told you might be."

"You don't even know me. I'm just some kid who's walked in. You never even seen me before."

"You match the description well enough, even allowing for the changes over the last three years."

I glance at the girl. If only she'd do something. With two of us we might be able to confuse him or something. He hasn't jumped on me yet and he could have. If it was just murder he wanted, he'd have rubbed me out by now.

Like he did Trixi.

I glance at her. She's gone. No doubt about it. I'm guessing he smashed her over the head with that chair. I look back to the gobbo.

"What did you kill her for? What's she done?"

"Who said I killed her?"

He's zipping me over. I know he killed her. I shout at the troll.

"Did he kill her?"

No answer. Don't think she's even heard me. She's just huddled there. Gobbo shakes his head.

"You can take that as a no."

"I'll take it as a yes."

He's not even listening. He's talking into a mobile.

"I've got him in the bungalow. How long will you be? . . . Okay, see you in five minutes."

He hangs up, gives me a little smile. I shout at the troll.

"Throw me your knife!"

Still nothing from her, not even a look. Gobbo speaks.

"I think that might be hard for her. I seem to have acquired it myself. When we had a little scuffle."

He pulls out a knife, gives me another smile.

That's it, Bigeyes. I didn't want to touch her but there's nothing else for it. I'm into Trixi's pockets and here's her knife first go. I pull it out, flick it open, turn back.

Gobbo's stiffened. He's watching me close. He should have jumped while I was looking away. Why hasn't he? He's wary, wary of a kid. But he's talking confident.

"That's my boy! Now I know you're who I thought you were."

Say nothing. Watch. Wait. Choose the moment. There'll only be one.

"You're the boy they call Blade," says the man.

"You're looking for someone else."

"The boy who's a wonder with a knife."

"You're looking for someone else. I never heard of a kid called Blade."

"But you're a wonder with a knife. Anyone can see that. Look at the way you're handling it. Like you could just throw that knife and hit anything you wanted."

"You better watch out, then, Scumbo."

"Oh, I'm watching out."

He is, too. He's talking big but his eyes are fixed on me. I can read his mind, Bigeyes. He's thinking the kid's got one shot with that knife. It could be lethal or he might miss. Too risky to take a chance, so wait till the other gobbos get here.

Sound of an engine outside the bungalow.

Gobbo gives me a gloaty look.

"We're going to take you to see some old friends. They're looking forward to catching up with you again. You'll have lots to talk about." He glances at the girl. "Unfortunately we're going to have to silence our companion. But we can't take any risks, I'm afraid. I'm sure you both understand."

Engine falls quiet. Crunch of car doors, two of 'em. The other gobbo and the grunt probably. Footsteps on the path. Got to do something, got to act now.

But the troll moves first.

She takes me by surprise, and the guy by the door. She's on her feet. She's choked out of her wits but she's making herself move. She yells at me.

"Throw the knife at him!"

Footsteps in the hall. I raise my arm to throw the knife. Gobbo does the same with his but I can see he's not comfortable. He's holding it all wrong. He can cream a knife off a girl but he's got no idea how to throw it.

But there's no time for either of us to throw.

The girl jumps across the bed, picks up the chair and hurls it at the window. The glass shatters and the chair carries through into the garden.

Gobbo shapes to throw again but the door opens behind him and knocks him down. I see the grunt glaring through at me from the hall.

"There he is!" he bawls.

Girl grabs me by the arm.

"Out the window!" she shouts, and dives through the gap.

I'm right behind her, still holding the knife. We roll over the grass and scramble to our feet.

"Run!" she says.

We're tearing across the garden. Over the fence, into the road. My arm's got a gash from the jagged glass. Footsteps behind us. I'm following the girl and she's running like the wind. If she was frozen before, she's fizzing now.

She's heading for the canal.

Don't know if it's a good idea. Don't know anything anymore. But there's no time to think. Got to run. Got to run, run, run.

14

So we run.

Onto the bridge, over the canal, down to the towpath. Left or right? She goes right, toward the city. I don't argue, just follow. We're haring down the towpath. Nobody about but she's made the right decision. We need people around us and the city's the place.

Check behind.

No sight of the grunt but the two gobbos have reached the bridge.

"Keep up!" says the girl.

I'm struggling. She's fast and I'm not. But we've got a head start on the gobbos and if we get to the end of the towpath quick enough, we should lose 'em. Girl glances back.

"Shit!" she says.

I see what she means. They're quicker than I thought. They're racing down after us, much quicker than me, quicker than the troll even. But here's the end of the towpath. We push through the gate.

"Head for Meadway Drive," I say.

"What for?"

"There's a building site, shops, people. We need people around us."

She cuts off toward Meadway Drive. The gobbos are much closer now, just a few yards from the gate, but we're over the street and tearing down Meadway Drive. There's the building site. Plenty of guys there already, and lots of nebs down the shopping parade, even some schoolkids. Look behind.

The gobbos have stopped. One's talking on a mobile. I touch the troll on the arm.

"They've stopped."

"I've seen," she says.

She carries on running and I do the same. She's right. We got to get well clear of them, got to put some distance between us.

We run on. I'm tired out now and she must be too, but I can see from her face she's still choked out. She's probably thinking of Trixi, and so am I.

I didn't like her, Bigeyes. I hated her. But I didn't want to see her dead, any more than I wanted to see Mary dead. If she is dead. I still don't know what happened to the old girl. Maybe the gobbos dumped her somewhere.

Some time or other I'm going to have to decide what to do. But one thing I know for certain.

I don't want to get mixed up with this troll. I got enough to think about, especially with these gobbos. They used my name. They're from the past, and that means trouble.

Playing dead hasn't worked.

The last thing I need is this troll hanging around. I've survived by staying alone. That's the only way to ride the dream. Stay alone. Then no one can touch you.

She's slowing down. I'm glad of that. I'm bombed out. I need to rest.

We're closer to the city center now. Loads of nebs around. No sign of danger but I'm checking about me real cute.

Cos everything's changed now. I've got to watch more

carefully than ever, and I've got to decide about this troll. But she's got ideas of her own.

"This way," she says.

She's heading down one of the alleyways toward the dockyard. Not a place I'm keen on. But at least the gobbos shouldn't find us down here.

I follow. Don't want to, Bigeyes. I want to split. But I've got to talk to this girl. I've got to find out what happened. And she might know about Mary.

But I don't like following other people. I like to go where I know I'm safe.

"Where are we going?"

She doesn't answer. I'm thinking about the other trolls now. I don't want 'em in my face again. But she's not looking for them. She's pulled around into a side alley.

I've seen this place before. Doesn't run through to anything, just a little cul-de-sac where drunks or druggies hang out. Sometimes you find the odd duff sleeping under a newspaper.

No one here now.

She slumps down, back against the wall, turns to the side.

And she's throwing up.

I can't deal with this, okay? I can't deal with it. I know she's choked out. I know she's lost her mate. But I can't be dealing with this. I've got to think of myself.

Don't look at me like that. I've got to think of myself. You understand? It's how I survive.

I'VE GOT TO THINK OF MYSELF.

I'm still standing there, looking down. She's gobbed all

over the ground and now she's retching with nothing coming up.

Don't know what to do.

What do I do, Bigeyes? Tell me what to do.

I bend down.

"You all right?"

She doesn't answer. Don't blame her. It was a stupid question.

She's stopped retching now. Pulls out a paper handkerchief, wipes her mouth, stands up, looks at me, anger in her eyes. Walks past me, stops a few yards away, slumps down again. Can't work this girl out.

"I'm moving away from the sick," she says.

"Oh."

Silence.

She's dropped her head, like she doesn't want to look at me. Obviously wants me to go. I start to walk past her.

"Stay," she says.

I stop, look down. She lifts her head just enough for me to see her eyes. They're still angry.

"Stay," she says.

I sit down next to her. She lights a cig, takes a few drags, offers it to me.

"No, thanks."

"Clean-living kid, are you?"

I don't answer.

"What did you do with the knife?" she says.

"I closed it up while we were running."

"Where is it?"

"In my pocket."

"Give it to me."

I look at her. Don't like those eyes. They scare me. She's out of her mind right now. She holds out her hand.

"Give it to me."

"What you going to do with it?"

"I ain't going to stick it in you if that's what you're worrying about."

I give her the knife.

She looks at it, flicks open the blade, starts crying. It makes her look young. She must be about sixteen like the other trolls in the gang. She looks like a little kid now.

But the tears don't last. She wipes them away, savagely, and then she's sixteen again. She stares at the knife, runs a finger along the edge.

"So that's your name, is it?" she says.

She looks up at me.

"Blade?"

15

MY NAME'S JONNY," I say.

"That guy called you Blade."

"He was mixing me up with someone else."

"He said you know how to handle a knife."

"I told you. He was mixing me up with someone else."

"You looked like you can handle a knife. When you was holding it. You looked like you've used a knife before."

"I was just pretending. Trying to scare him."

"So you're called Jonny?"

"Yeah."

"And what are you called when you're not lying?"

"Jonny."

"I'm calling you Blade."

I don't want her to, Bigeyes. I don't want that name getting around. I told you the name but you're the only one I've told it to since I came to the city.

It's a name from my old life.

It's the name Becky gave me, so it's special. Cos Becky was special. I don't want this troll using it. I look back at her.

"So what's your name?"

"Becky."

Shit, Bigeyes, this is going from bad to worse. And she's not zipping me over. She's telling the truth. I can always tell. She's called Becky. She's bloody called Becky.

"I'm calling you Blade," she says again.

"I don't give two bells what you call me."

"Two what?"

"Never mind."

"You talk funny."

"I talk like I talk."

She's not listening. She's crying again. She's like loads of things all at once now. Angry, sad, frightened, defiant. A little kid and a fighting troll.

And she's still holding the knife.

I'm watching it. Whatever she said about not sticking it in me, I'm watching that knife.

"Becky?"

Feels funny saying her name. She doesn't answer, just goes on crying those angry tears.

"Becky? What happened in the bungalow?"

She's looking around at me. Eyes wet, cheeks wet. I'm telling you, she's right on the edge. I've got to watch everything she does. She wipes her eyes with her sleeve, glares at me, answers.

"We went in, me and Trix. It was a test."

"What kind of test?"

"A test for me. To see if I had the bottle."

"For the gang?"

"Yeah. I'm on the outside, right? I'm not one o' them. I ain't proved myself. They think."

It sounds right. I recognized the other five trolls. Didn't recognize this one. And she hung back a bit when they sorted me on the towpath. Just a bit.

She still got in a couple of kicks.

"So it was a test?"

"Yeah. Trixi's been watching the bungalow. She's wanted to break in for ages."

"What for? There's nothing much in there."

"It's not about nicking stuff."

"So what is it about?"

"It's about doing some damage. She don't like the people who live there. The guy mouthed her off once for making a noise in the street. His wife joined in too. And their son's a greasy little snipe. So it's personal."

I'm listening hard, Bigeyes. A guy, she said. A wife, a son. Nothing about old Mary.

"So what happened?" I say.

"Trix told us she'd seen 'em leave the house, all packed up like they was off on holiday. And we was all set to go in the next day. But we found some old girl with a dog hanging around there. So we had to wait."

"Who was she?"

"Don't know."

"Then what?"

"Day after we done you on the towpath, Trix tells me we're going in, just her and me. Says the old woman's gone and I got to break in with her. Says I got to nick some stuff and mess the place up but not leave no prints or nothing."

"Why just you? Why not the other girls?"

"Cos she knows I'm scared, specially of the police."

"Why?"

"None of your business."

She gives me another glare. I'm not arguing. She's got the knife and I haven't.

"So you went in. You and Trix."

"Yeah, only I knew something was wrong. Front door was smashed already. You seen it yourself. We just walked in. And Trix tells me to check out the spare bedroom while she does the main bedroom."

I know where this is going, Bigeyes. I can see it already. She doesn't need to tell me any more.

"So I check out the spare room. Nothing much there. And I walk through into the main bedroom and . . ."

She seizes up again. She's not crying this time. She's shaking and retching again, and she's squeezing the hilt of the knife like she wants to crush it. I want to take it off her but I don't dare. If I touch her, she'll round on me. I just know.

"Easy," I say.

She doesn't hear me.

"Becky? Easy."

"Shut up!"

I shut up. Too right I shut up. Let her get through it. I don't need any more anyway. She's told me enough. I can guess the rest.

Maybe I could go. I want to go. I don't want any more of this.

But I can't move.

Don't ask me why.

She's stopped retching. She's still shaking and she's staring at me with those . . . those eyes. She takes a slow breath.

"I walked into the main bedroom, and there's Trixi lying on the floor. I don't know why I didn't hear nothing. I mean, no scream. No . . . thump when he hit her. Maybe I was just too scared to notice stuff. I just wanted to run."

"Then what?"

"This hand grabbed me from behind the door. I pulled out my knife but he wrenched it straight off me."

She's gripping the knife and biting her knuckles at the same time.

"I tried to fight him but he knocked me about so hard I just . . . lost it. I crumpled up. The girls are right. I got no fight in me. Trixi wouldn't have given up. If she hadn't been hit first, she'd have given him some grief."

"How long were you in there before I turned up?"

"Don't know. Couple of minutes, maybe more. Seemed longer."

"Were you really scared or were you playing scared?"

"I was really scared. Then when you started answering him back, I got some bottle and went for it."

Her face has changed again. It's got something else, something new. She's right. She's not like the other trolls. I don't know what it is. But there's something they've got that she hasn't. And something she's got that they haven't.

It's in her face right now.

I'm getting in too deep, Bigeyes. And I don't want to.

As for Mary, I don't know much more than I did. Except I was right. She doesn't live in that bungalow.

I look hard at Becky. "What are you going to do about Trixi?"

She looks angrily back at me. "You mean, what are *we* going to do about Trixi?"

"No. What are *you* going to do about Trixi?"

"I'll leave a message with the police. But I'm not giving my name."

"They'll come for you anyway. They must know your gang. And you got a criminal record, right?"

"I been in a bit of trouble."

"Like what?"

"Like none of your business."

Fair enough. Can't say I blame her. I'm keeping my secrets too.

"They'll find you," I say. "One of the gang'll give you away. Specially as they know you went off with Trixi. You'll be the major suspect."

"That's why I ain't going to the police station. I'll ring 'em up and tell 'em about the men."

"Are you going to tell 'em about me?"

She stands up suddenly.

"Depends," she says.

"On what?"

She closes the knife and puts it in her pocket.

"Come with me," she says.

16

I DON'T KNOW WHY I'M FOLLOWING HER. Maybe I'm worried.

Okay, I am worried. I admit it. I don't like being seen, or recognized anyway. Now these nebs have turned up from the past and if this troll starts talking to the police about me, they'll start hunting as well. And they'll start looking through their records for stuff. They'll find their way right back to where I don't want 'em to go.

I got to stop her from talking about me to anyone.

And that means some kind of deal. I don't know what she wants but she wants something. I've got to find out what it is. She doesn't waste any time telling me.

"I want a doss," she says.

She's walking fast down another one of the alleyways. We're going parallel to the dockyard, out of sight of the river. I'm struggling to keep up.

"What you asking me for?" I say.

"Cos you got somewhere to sleep."

"You don't know that."

"Yeah, I do." She glances at me. "You're smart. I can tell. You're sharp as they come. No wonder they call you Blade."

"I told you—the guy was thinking of someone else."

"He wasn't. He was thinking of you. You're Blade."

We walk on down the alleyway.

"You don't know my name," I say. "Neither did Trixi. I never told any of your gang my name."

She looks at me again.

"You know why Trixi called you Slicky?"

"No."

"That was her name for you. Cos of the way you look. She used to say you're too slick to be a street thief. You don't sleep rough. Anyone can see that. You're always clean. You've always got nice clothes on. Well, not right now."

"Thanks to you."

"Trix wanted to sort you proper. She didn't like you working our streets and poncing about in flash clothes."

"They weren't flash. They were just tidy."

"They were that, all right. You look like you come from some nice home with a nice mummy and daddy and a nice big car and a dog and a cat and lots of money."

"Maybe I do."

She gives a funny little laugh, kind of giggly. Makes her sound like a kid again. But the eyes soon harden and the years pile back on.

"You ain't got a home like that," she says. "You're a loner. You're drifting around the city same as me. You ain't got no one here. Have you?"

"None of your business."

We reach the end of the alleyway and stop. She's looking me over again. I can't handle this, Bigeyes. It's banging me out. I got enough to think about with those gobbos and all this stuff from the past coming back. I don't need this girl's rubble too.

"You're drifting," she says.

"That's what Trixi told you, is it?"

"Trixi? She thought you were some jumped-up rich kid lifting wallets for fun and then going back to a nice rich home. That's why she hated you. You weren't nicking stuff cos you needed it. You were nicking stuff cos it was a laugh. All the girls thought that."

"Except you."

"Yeah." She sniffs. "Except me."

"You might all be wrong. I might have a home. And I might not be a rich kid."

She leans close. I move back. She stops, but she's still watching me.

"Jumpy, ain't you?" she says. "What did you think I was going to do?"

I don't answer.

"I ain't got the knife open," she says. "It's in my pocket. What did you think I was going to do?"

Don't answer. Just watch. She's staring back at me, like she doesn't know what to make of me. She straightens up.

"You're not a rich kid. And you ain't got no home. But you got a doss."

Don't answer. Just watch.

"You got a doss," she says. "And I want to share it. One night, that's all. One night and I'm away. Let me stay there tonight and I won't say nothing about you to the police. I'll tell 'em about Trixi and the man and what happened. But I won't say nothing about you."

"If I find you a doss for tonight."

"If you find me a doss for tonight."

"But you must have been dossing somewhere till now."

"I have. But I can't go back there. Not now. The girls'll find me. The police'll find me."

"They'll find you anyway."

"Not if I'm gone."

"Go now, then."

She shakes her head, looks down.

"I ain't eaten for three days. The gang was giving me stuff but not much. Trixi said I had to prove myself before they'd give me anything more. I can't nick money like you do. I'm no good at it. I'd get caught first go. And now this thing with Trixi."

She looks up again.

"The girls'll kill me. They don't like me anyway. They don't trust me. They'll think I walked out on Trixi. It won't make no difference what I tell 'em. They'll think I ran for it and let Trixi get killed. They won't even listen. And if the police get me, they'll send me back."

"Back where?"

She says nothing but she doesn't need to. Her face is a story I don't want to read.

I don't know what to do, Bigeyes. I need this troll off my back. And how do I know she'll do what she says? She could shunt me anyway, even if I do help her. But not helping her might be a bigger risk.

"Come with me," I say.

She shakes her head.

"You got to come with me first," she says.

"I'm not going anywhere with you. You want a doss, so you come with me. I lead the way."

She moves so quick I don't have to time to run. One moment she's standing there, the next she's pushed me back against the wall and the knife's out and open and pricking against my throat.

"Shit, Becky! Lay off!"

"Listen." Her voice is like distant thunder. "We got a deal. You find me a doss for the night, and some food, and I'm out of your life in the morning. I'll come with you. I'll follow. But first you got to come with me. You got to agree to come with me."

"What for?"

The knife moves slowly over my throat. I look all the way down it and up into Becky's eyes. They're midnight black.

"There's someone coming with us," she says.

17

WE'RE WALKING ON. Alleyways well behind us, docks open on the left. Lighters, barges, river slinking by. It's gray and dark, not interested in us. Too busy moving.

Same as the people. Lots of nebs around here but they're just like the river. Moving, moving, moving. I don't like coming this way. Still can't believe I'm following this troll.

She keeps looking over her shoulder, like to check I'm here.

Why am I here, Bigeyes?

I should be gone. It's hardly difficult. I could wig it easy as kissing air. She couldn't stop me with all these nebs around. I didn't even give my word. She took my look as my word but I never gave it.

Maybe I would have given it if she'd pushed me. I mean, she had the knife against my throat and I'm going to agree to anything with that thing stuck there, aren't I? But it's not there now. It's back in her pocket.

So why aren't I gone?

Docks coming to an end but she's carrying on past the derricks and warehouses. River twists away here, opens up and gulps in the sea. I don't come here much. Sea scares me just looking at it. I hate the thing.

Just as well Becky's turned away from it.

She's heading right, back into the city, toward the Hedley estate. I can see the park and playing fields, the first scattering of houses. She's taking me down one of the paths that skirt the cricket pitch.

Quite a few nebs here too but they're all muffins.

Becky's fallen silent. I'm glad of that. I need to think. I need to work out what to do. I don't have to help her. Like I said, just cos she thinks I agreed doesn't mean I did agree. I don't know why I'm hesitating. I wouldn't normally. I'd just blast off out of here.

Maybe it's the name.

Becky.

Why's she got to be called that? She's nothing like my Becky. She never could be. Nobody could be. Except in the name. But maybe that's it. Maybe that's why I'm still following.

Past the cricket pitch, down Maddison Crescent, around the shopping parade, over the railway bridge, down the path alongside the track. Becky speaks for the first time since we left the alleyway.

"Blade?"

She's glancing over her shoulder, still walking. I can see her eyes, black as before.

"I'm not called Blade."

"Yes, you are," she says.

"What do you want?"

"You know the Hedley estate?"

Do I know the Hedley estate? Better than she does, Bigeyes, that's for sure. I know every bit of this city. I bet she doesn't.

"What about it?"

"There's a house we've got to go to." She frowns. "But I don't want to go in."

"You got a problem, then."

"I want you to go in for me."

"That's tough cos I won't."

She stops and turns but this time I'm ready for her. I'm already two steps back. But she doesn't come for me with the knife. She hasn't even pulled it out. She's just standing there, her mouth quivering.

I still don't trust her. Anyone can put on tears. She cried earlier but that was genuine. She was choked out over Trixi. This is different. Don't ask me how I know.

Her mouth stops moving. No tears but she's not right. She's watching me close. I'm watching her close too, as cute as I can. She could do anything right now. She doesn't move but she speaks.

"She's in a house on the estate."

"Who?"

"Jaz."

"Who's Jaz?"

"My daughter."

"Your what?"

"It's short for Jasmine."

"I don't give two bells what it's short for. How come you got a daughter? And what about—"

"There's no father." She shrugs. "Well, there's a father. Obviously there's a father but he's . . ." She shrugs again. "He's nowhere. Gone. It's just me an' Jaz. She's only three. I was thirteen when I had her. And I got to get her out of that house."

"Then you can go and get her by yourself. It's nothing to do with me."

She gives me this hard look.

"Get her for me and I won't tell the police about you."

"Hold on. We had a deal. A doss and some food. Nothing about a kid."

"I told you someone was coming with us."

"You didn't say anything about me going to get her."

"Well, that's the deal."

Got to think, Bigeyes. Got to think fast. Nothing to stop me from running. But what if she does tell the police about me? I've been playing dead for three years. I've been safe under the radar and I want to stay there. Specially now that those gobbos have turned up. If the porkers get onto me again, they'll make things even worse.

Not that I trust this troll to honor her word. I could fetch her kid and get them both a doss and some food, and she could still shunt me later with the police. I'll take a risk with her but there's something I need to know first.

"What's with this house? Why can't you go and get her?"

She looks me over.

"Some of the gang might be there."

"They got a house?"

"It's not theirs. It belongs to Tammy's gran. You know Tammy?"

"I know what her nails feel like in my face."

"She and Sash were Trixi's favorites. They both hate me. But Tammy's gran's been letting me doss there sometimes and leave Jaz with her while I'm out with the gang."

"You been leaving your kid with an old woman you don't even know?"

"She's all right. I mean, she's stoned half the time but she's quite kind. She wouldn't do Jaz no harm. And anyway, she's never the only person there. There's always other people at the house."

She looks away, like she wishes she hadn't just said that. I give her a prompt.

"Like who?"

She doesn't look back. She's hesitating and I know why. She knows I won't go in if it's too dangerous. And I'm telling you—she's right.

"Like who?"

She looks back at me.

"Like . . . people. People the gang know. They just use the place to hang out."

Use the old woman more like. I can see it clear enough.

"I can't go in," she says. "They'll ask questions."

"You could tell 'em the truth. Just leave out the bit about me. You saw Trixi dead. You struggled with the guy. Threw the chair out the window. Ran away."

"They won't believe me."

"So how do you expect me to get your kid out?"

She leans closer again. I move back, keep the distance there. She stops, watching my face. She's being careful, Bigeyes. I can see that. She's trying not to push her luck. Even her voice is softer.

"You're smart," she says. "I told you before. You're dead smart. You ain't fast when it comes to running but your mind's quick. There's something about you. I seen your eyes moving as you walk. You don't miss nothing. You're used to staying out of sight. And you can handle yourself."

She pulls the knife out of her pocket but doesn't flick it open.

"Take it," she says.

I don't take it.

She reaches out and drops it in my pocket.

"Jaz'll be in one of two places. There's a little shed at the bottom of the garden. She likes to play in there. She calls it her den. Or she'll be in the lounge. She usually sits in the corner and draws."

I'm hating the picture I've got in my head now. I can see it clear and it's fizzing me out. I don't want anything to do with it. Though I'll tell you, Bigeyes, and I don't really understand it, but I'm starting to feel something for this kid.

Jaz, I mean.

First she's got a mum like Becky. That's bad enough. Then she's stuck with an old dunny who's stoned out of her head. Not to mention the other nebs who keep turning up.

I can guess what they're like.

"So if she's in the shed, we're lucky, and if she's in the lounge, we're not. Is that what you're saying?"

I can't believe I'm even asking this. Becky's quick with a reply.

"Yeah, but we can still get her even if she's in the lounge. We just got to watch the house and wait for our chance. If she's in the lounge on her own, you could tap on the window, get her to open it and tell her she's just got to climb out and come with you."

"Oh, yeah, like she's going to do that with a stranger."

"She will. I'll give you something from me, something she'll recognize. Say it's from Fairypops."

"Eh?"

"Fairypops. We got little names for each other. She's Fairybell. I'm Fairypops."

"This isn't happening."

"Just say it. She'll believe you. She's dead trusting with people."

"Haven't taught her much, then, have you?"

Becky's mouth tightens.

"I teach her what I can but she still trusts people, okay? That's how she is. Don't matter if I warn her about someone. She just trusts."

Now it's me looking away. I can't face this troll right now. What do I do, Bigeyes? Tell me—what do I do?

Just trusts. What kind of a person just trusts? Even kids can't be that stupid, can they?

I look back at Becky.

"Let's go."

18

I KNOW THIS HOUSE. I knew it even when Becky was talking about it. The moment she mentioned a shed in the garden. There's a few of those around here but only one that a kid would use as a den.

I could have done with a shed like that when I was three.

Look at it. Proper little snug tucked away behind the apple tree. Not like the house. Pothole of a place, isn't it? If only the kid was in the den right now, we'd be all right. Trouble is, she's not. Don't ask me how I know.

Becky's fidgeting.

"Blade?"

"What?"

"Come on. We're wasting time. The gang's not there. It's just the old girl. See the upstairs window? She's in the bedroom."

"I've seen her. I'm looking for the girl."

"You got to try the shed first."

"She's not in there."

"You don't know. You haven't looked."

"She's not in there."

"The door's ajar. I can see it from here."

"So what?"

"So she could be inside."

I'm not answering. I can't be wasting time over this. I'm watching the house. The old dunny's still upstairs. I recognize her now. Seen her a few times around these streets. Didn't know she lived here though. Didn't know Trixi's gang used the house either. They usually work the east side.

Just shows how you got to keep watching.

Remember what I said, Bigeyes? You got to watch the city all the time, watch her as cute as you can. That's how you stay alive.

Dunny's moving. Away from the window, lost her, back again, downstairs, into the kitchen, out again, into the lounge. Slumps in the armchair. She looks bombed out.

Check around. Dronky houses, dronky gardens, dogs barking, radio on next door. Some gobbo arguing with his missus in the house opposite. Least this path's deserted and we've got a clear view of the house through the gaps in the fence.

Becky's talking again.

"Come on, Blade. Let's go."

"I thought you didn't want to go in."

"I've changed my mind. It's just the old girl and she's half gone. But we'll check the shed first."

"She's not there. I told you."

"We'll check the shed. If she ain't there, we'll do the house."

"No."

I'm scowling at her. Don't know why. This is her business. She should be sorting it anyway. But there's something chipping inside my head, something about this house, something Becky won't handle.

"No," I say.

"No what?"

"I'll do it."

She's staring at me.

"I'm better at this than you," I say.

"Meaning?"

"Meaning I'm better at this than you. You're not used to creeping around houses."

"How do you know?"

"I just do. And anyway—there's something not right about the house."

"Like what?"

"Like I don't know. But there's something not right."

She doesn't answer.

"Wait here," I tell her. "I'll bring her out."

"All right, but give her this."

She pulls something out of her pocket. Fluffy thing, dead tiny. Gives it to me.

"Peter Rabbit," I say.

He fits right inside my hand.

"Who's Peter Rabbit?" she says.

"Don't you ever read?"

"No, do you?"

Do I ever read, Bigeyes? If only she knew.

I put the little rabbit inside my pocket.

"So that's for Jaz?"

"Yeah. Tell her you're a friend. Tell her Fairypops is waiting outside for her." Becky looks back at the house. "This is stupid. I should be going in with you."

"No, stay here and keep out of sight."

I'm gone. Got to move now before she argues any more. Just hope she stays put. She could mess everything up. I need to keep sharp. I can't be watching for her as well.

Over the fence, across the grass, against the wall.

Listen, watch. Radio still going next door. House opposite's gone quiet but there's children shouting somewhere down the street. Bounce of a soccer. No sound from the dunny's house but that means nothing. Something's wrong here. Something I can't see. And Becky's right about one thing.

There's no time to waste.

Peep around the window. Dunny's still slumped in the chair. No one else in the room. Check around. No windows overlooking me from here but the front door's exposed. Around toward the back, stop by the kitchen window, check around.

Empty.

Knew it would be. The kid's upstairs but that's where the trouble is too. I can sense it. Past the kitchen, stop, check. Only one window overlooking me and that's the house on the other side of the garden but there's no one watching.

Around to the back door, stop, check again.

Nobody watching.

Thump of the soccer down the street, a crash, a shout, sound of laughter, running feet.

Silence.

Open the door, listen.

Not a sound inside the house.

Into the kitchen, through the hall, soft, soft. Stop by the lounge. Door's half open. Check through the gap. Dunny's head's drooping on her chest, cig burning in the ashtray. Up the stairs, softer now, softer than ever. This is where it gets hard. Smell of gin, dope, mold. Stop on the landing.

Check around.

Three doors, two open. Poky little bedrooms, nobody in

'em. Stop by the third. Got to be the bathroom. Why's the door closed? Ear to it, listen long.

Nothing.

She's got to be in there. Question is, who else is?

Check back down the stairs. May need to wig it fast. But I'm not going without Jaz. Don't ask me why. I don't know either. But I'm not going without her.

Squeeze the door handle, turn, push. It's not locked. Open the door, just a bit. No sound inside. Push a bit more. Door catches on something. It's someone's foot.

No one speaks.

Head around the door.

Cloud of smoke, can't see in. I make myself step over the threshold—and now it's clear. There's nebs crowded in the room.

Big, fat gobbo lying in the bath, naked as a whale. Woman slumped against the toilet, two guys sprawled next to her. Needles and syringes in the basin.

Piece of paper on the floor, far corner. Pencil lying on top. A drawing, a kid's drawing. I can see it from here. A little bird.

Only there's no kid.

Suddenly the door slams behind me. One of the guys has kicked it shut. He's sitting up, drilling me with his eyes.

"Who are you?" he says.

I squeeze the fluffy rabbit in my pocket.

"Jaz's Uncle Peter."

"Eh?"

"Jaz's Uncle Peter."

They're all stirring now, even the gobbo in the bath. Big,

misty faces. Never seen 'em before but they look like duffs off the street. Woman glances at me.

"You don't look like much of an uncle. More like a turd off the pavement."

Gobbos all laugh.

I look around at the nebs. They're all staring at me. Guy who kicked the door shut's blocking it with his foot. Shows no sign of moving. I look into his eyes. They're still drilling me. He gives a little smirk.

"All right, Uncle Peter?"

"Where's Jaz?"

"Not here."

"I noticed that. Where is she?"

Gobbo glances at his mates.

"Not very polite, is he?"

Another laugh. I try something different.

"Her mum's looking for her."

"Ah, bless," says the woman.

I look at her. She's the only one here'll tell me. But I got to handle her right.

"Cute kid, isn't she?" I say.

"Yeah."

The woman's eyes are like dusk falling. I lean closer to her.

"Any idea where she is, darling?"

"I ain't your darling, you little gobshite."

"Yeah, right. Any idea where she is?"

"She run out when we come in. Left her picture behind her. Try the bedroom."

I looked in both bedrooms, Bigeyes. But maybe . . .

I step over to the far corner, pick up the drawing and the pencil, walk back to the door. The gobbo's still got his foot against it. I squeeze the fluffy rabbit in my pocket, let go, feel for the knife, lock my fingers around it.

Long time since I carried a knife for real. Even longer since I used one.

I think of Trixi and Mary, and Jaz, and then this smirking dungpot. I'm staring hard at him now, drilling him back. He's noticed the difference in my face. I can tell from his manner. His eyes are flickering downward. He's watching my hand move inside the pocket.

He smirks again, then shifts his leg, just enough.

I open the door, listen, check around, slip out to the landing. The bedroom, she said. Which one? Could be either. Try the one on the right first.

Creep in, close the door behind me. Nobody to be seen, but I got an idea now. Down on my knees, check under the bed, and there she is—a little girl peering out.

Face like a snowdrop.

She doesn't move, doesn't scream, doesn't do anything, just looks at me with those big eyes. I give her a smile, whisper.

"Hey, Jaz. You forgot your picture."

I hold it out to her. She doesn't take it, just looks at it, then back at me.

"Great drawing," I say. "You going to finish it, sweetheart?"

"Ain't got no pencil."

"Here it is. I brought it."

I show her the pencil.

"I can't draw under 'ere," she says.

"Come on out, then."

She crawls out, takes the picture and the pencil. I touch the paper.

"It's lovely, Jaz. What is it, a thrush?"

"Robin."

"You need a bit of red for the breast, don't you?"

"Ain't got no red."

"I'll fix that for you. Listen, guess who sent me."

She doesn't answer. I lower my voice.

"Fairypops. She's waiting outside. Shall we go and see her? We can finish the picture later."

I stand up, hold out my hand. Jaz gets up without a word and takes it. Then she looks at me.

"Where's Rabbit?"

"Here." I pull him out. "He's been missing you."

She doesn't take him.

"Don't you want him, Jaz?"

"Got to carry the picture."

"Do you want me to carry Rabbit?"

"Yeah."

"Okay, let's go."

I walk her toward the door. Got to get her out of here quick. I don't like what I'm feeling in this place. But now there's another problem.

Voices downstairs.

19

Some of the trolls are back. Not sure how many. I can hear Tammy and a couple of others. No sound of Sash.

I open the door a fraction, listen. Voices still there, downstairs, but they've moved into the lounge. I glance back at Jaz.

"Come on."

She doesn't argue, doesn't even look worried. Becky's right. The kid just trusts. It's scary how much she trusts. I lead her out of the bedroom, ease her to the side of the landing so we're out of view of downstairs.

Listen again.

Tammy's voice. She's talking to the old dunny, extra loud.

"Gran? You listening to me?"

Dunny says nothing. I squeeze Jaz by the hand, lean down, whisper.

"Jaz? Do you want to play a game?"

She looks up at me, says nothing, then nods. I lean closer.

"We got to be dead quiet. We got to sneak out the house without anyone seeing us or hearing us. Can you do that?"

She nods again.

"Good girl. We'll sneak out the house and go and find Fairypops. But you got to be dead quiet. Not a word, not a sound, okay?"

She nods a third time. Tammy's still raging downstairs.

"Gran, for Christ's sake! Have you seen her?"

This time a murmur back.

"Who?"

"Trixi! Has she been here?"

"No, dear."

"What about Becky?"

Don't catch an answer this time but now there's a bang at the door, and a rush of feet, and then the door swinging open and Sash's voice.

"She's dead!"

An explosion of shouts. They're all gabbling at once but Sash is pouring out the story.

"She's in that bungalow by the towpath. She must have took Becky with her. I went in and found her in the bedroom. She's been smashed over the head."

"What about Becky?" says Tammy.

"Not there. But listen." Sash is breathing hard. I can hear it from upstairs. She goes on. "I seen her. She didn't see me but I seen her. On my way to the bungalow, I seen her running down Meadway Drive. She was running toward the docks. And you know who she was with?"

"Who?"

"Slicky."

There's a buzz from downstairs. The old dunny's trying to speak, something about calling the police. The trolls aren't listening and neither am I. I'm looking about me, trying to find a way out.

They're still in the lounge. If we go down now, we might just be able to slip out without being seen. Cos in a moment they're going to come and check for Jaz. They'll know Becky's got to come back for her. I give her another whisper.

"Ready, Jaz?"

But now the bathroom door opens.

The gobbo from the bath's standing there, still naked, dripping water all over the floor. He slopes out onto the landing and stands there, swaying. I pull Jaz closer but his eyes don't even notice us. The woman steps out too, then the other two gobbos. The naked guy bellows down the stairs.

"Can you people stop that damned infernal row?"

Got a posh mouth for a duff and it's the last thing we need. Tammy's already out of the lounge and shouting up at him.

"Get out of here! We've told you before! Get out!"

In a minute she'll be up the stairs and then she'll see us. I glance back toward the bedroom. There's just a chance. . . .

The naked guy's answering back in that same plummy voice.

"We're here by right, young woman. Your grandmother was kind enough to invite us."

I lean down to Jaz. She hasn't moved, hasn't said a word, hasn't let go of my hand. Her face is watching mine. I whisper.

"Come with me."

Into the bedroom, slow, soft. Check behind, but nobody's watching us. The nebs are shouting down the stairs and the trolls are shouting up. I close the door, let go of Jaz's hand, top sheet off the bed, bottom sheet, tie 'em together, tie the end to the bedpost, open the window, throw out the sheet.

This might not work.

But it's got to.

"Jaz, listen."

She's looking up at me with those eyes.

"Jaz, you got to do what I say. I'm going to sit you on my shoulders and you're going to hang on to my head. And we're going to climb down to the garden. Can you do that?"

She nods.

I can't believe this kid. You just say something and she does it.

More shouts. Tammy's getting heated up. It's time to go. I test the end of the sheet, check out the window.

"Now, Jaz."

Lift her on my shoulders, legs either side of my head. She's as light as a feather. Just as well. She's got the drawing pushed against my face.

"Can we leave the picture behind, Jaz?"

"No."

"Okay."

No point arguing.

"Hold on tight."

She holds on, her hands and the picture clasped over my eyes. I can hardly see but I can feel my way. Leg over the window frame, hands on the sheet, other leg over the edge. Sheet's holding fine. Now down, easy, easy. Sheet's holding, girl's holding. We're on the ground.

"Good girl." I put her down. "Let's go and find Fairypops."

I take her hand, lead her to the back of the house. Voices still shouting inside. Check out the garden. On the other side of the fence I can see the top of Becky's head. She's moved around toward the shed at the bottom and she's seen us. She's beckoning us toward a little gate.

Stupid troll.

She's got no idea. I told her to keep out of sight and stay where she was, and here she is waving at us like a claphead. Anyone can see her from the house. There's nothing for it. We'll have to wig it to the gate before she does something even worse.

"Come on, Jaz. Run with me. Fast as you can."

We haven't gone ten yards before there's a shout behind us.

"You!"

It's the old dunny. She's leaning out the lounge window pointing at us.

"Stop!"

Tammy's face appears, sees us, disappears. A moment later she's tearing around the side of the house toward us, followed by Sash and the other two trolls.

They're all carrying knives.

20

We'll never get away, not with Jaz slowing us down. The only chance is to get among people so the girls can't do too much. Becky's screaming for Jaz.

"Jaz, come here!"

I give the kid a push.

"Run to Fairypops!"

Jaz runs to the gate. Becky's already got it open. She calls out to me too.

"Come on!"

I'm waiting just a bit to give the trolls more to think about. They've already slowed, like they're not sure whether to go for me or Becky and the kid. Dunny's still peering out the window. They probably won't do much here, not with her watching.

I glance around. Jaz is through the gate and Becky's got her. I catch her eyes.

"Come on!" she says.

I run to the gate, push through, pull it closed. Becky's picked up Jaz now. The kid's still clutching her picture. But here's Tammy and the others rushing the gate.

"Let's go!" says Becky.

She sets off down the path but she's running toward Hedley Woods.

"Becky! The other way! Into the city!"

We need people, not trees, but it's too late now. She's off

down the path and the trolls are nearly on me. I turn and race after her but I'm choking, Bigeyes, I'm choking bad. We're in the grime and it's Becky's fault.

I should leave her to it but I know I can't, not with Jaz. I can't just blast off. But we're never going to handle four trolls. We can't fight 'em and we can't outrun 'em. Becky could outrun 'em on her own but not carrying Jaz. I've caught her up already.

And the trolls are close behind.

Here are the woods. They don't go far and if we stick to the path and run fast enough, we might meet some people on the way. But Becky's already branched off into the trees.

"Becky! Get back on the path!"

"No! We can lose 'em in the trees!"

"Get back on the path!"

She's not listening. She's running blind. We're blundering among oaks and beeches—and then suddenly she stops, turns, stares. It's like she's suddenly realized there's no point. She's still holding Jaz and they're both looking past me.

I stop too, turn and look.

They're coming toward us, all four, not hurrying now that they've seen we've stopped. They're spreading out to cut off any escape. I stay where I am. No point in moving. I glance around.

Becky's moved back a few feet. She's put Jaz down and the two of them are standing by an old cedar. The little girl's still clutching her drawing. Doesn't look worried at all.

I wish I was her.

But I'm not. I'm me. Try as I might, I'm always me.

The trolls have stopped a few yards from me. I'm watching them but I can sense Becky and Jaz still standing behind me. I can sense the cedar tree even as I watch the faces before me.

Who's the worst now that Trixi's gone?

Hard to tell. Tammy and Sash are bad enough. Can't remember the names of the other two. But I've seen 'em enough times. I know what they can do.

Becky calls out.

"Xen! Kat! You don't have to do what Tammy tells you!"

"Shut it!" says the black-haired girl.

"Xen—!"

"I said shut it!"

Becky tries the other girl.

"Kat, listen—"

"Don't even bother," comes the answer.

And Becky falls silent.

So that's what they're called, Xen and Kat. But that's about as friendly as we're ever going to get. I'm watching Tammy. She's the nearest and she's clearly taken the lead. They're moving forward again. I give a shout.

"Stay back!"

"Shut your mouth, Slicky!" says Tammy.

"Stay back!"

"Going to stop us, are you?"

And that's when it happens.

That's the moment when I stop playing dead. One moment I'm a ghost, the next I'm standing there and the knife's out of my pocket and in my hand and the blade's open.

The girls stop, stare, glance at each other, back at me.

"Got a knife, Slicky?" says Sash. "Know how to use it?"

"Becky didn't kill Trix," I say. "Neither did I."

"Who did?"

Becky calls out behind me.

"Some guy. He was in the bungalow. I checked out one of the rooms while Trix checked out the main bedroom. I went in and found her lying dead. And this guy. He must have hit her over the head."

I'm watching the trolls, one face at a time. They don't believe a word of this.

"It's true," I say. "I saw him."

Tammy looks me up and down.

"You just happened to be there as well."

"Yeah."

She takes a step closer.

"So how come you're holding Trixi's knife?"

The other trolls stiffen. Tammy glances around at them.

"Didn't you notice?" she says to them. "Slicky's got her knife."

"I pulled it out of her pocket," I say. "To defend myself against the guy."

"It's true," says Becky.

But we're wasting our time. There's no point saying any more.

Sash is moving close too, and Xen, and Kat. Tammy snarls.

"You both had it in for Trix. Slicky cos of what we done on the towpath, and Bex cos Trixi told her she's yellow. But to take her out when she wasn't looking—"

"We didn't," says Becky.

But it's too late for words now. They're coming forward. I hold up the knife, shout at them.

"Stay back!"

They come on. Behind me I feel Becky and Jaz moving by the tree.

"Stay back or—"

"Or what?" says Sash.

I glance over my shoulder. Becky and Jaz are still standing by the cedar, the little girl clutching her picture.

"Or what?" Sash says again.

And suddenly I'm shouting to the kid.

"Jaz, hold up your picture so we can see it! Hold it above your head!"

And without a word, without a murmur, she does what she always does. She does as she's told. She holds the picture above her head. Just an inch or two above. But it's enough.

Cos already my arm's whipping through the air. Only for me it's like slow motion. I'm seeing the past and the present and all time spinning as the knife flies through the air, the point racing toward the little girl standing by the tree. And I'm watching her face. It's just looking back, quiet and still, the quietest, stillest place in this whole stinking world.

The knife thuds into the picture and pins it to the tree.

The robin struck through the heart.

And I'm running over to Jaz. She's as still as before, as quiet and trusting as she ever was. Becky's screaming at me but I've got no time for her. I tug the knife free and the picture flutters to the ground. I turn and face the trolls. They haven't moved. They're staring. I feel Jaz take my free hand.

Becky falls silent.

I call out to the trolls.

"First person who comes forward gets the same."

"Like Trixi got?" shouts Tammy.

"Not by me. Not by Becky."

They go on staring, long, hard, then slowly turn and head off back through the woods. Becky touches me on the arm.

"It's not over," she says.

I glance down at Jaz, her hand still in mine.

"It's just beginning," I say.

21

It's not the best snug in the world, Bigeyes, but it'll do for tonight. And being a flat, we can take a risk with the lights. Some of them anyway. Bedroom's okay, so's the lounge. There's dimmer switches in those rooms and the windows face out over the ring road. No one to see us but passing cars and we're too high up for anyone to care much about us.

Becky's been quiet all day. Hardly said a thing since we left the woods. Jaz doesn't say much either. Bit miffed that I messed up her picture but not for long. Keeps holding my hand.

Don't know where the rest of today's gone. Walking and watching, that's all I remember. And now it's eight in the evening, and it's dark, and my life's upside-down again.

It was good playing dead. I was sleeping my life out and it was sweet. I told you life's a whack. Trouble is, it's only a whack when you're in control. Rest of the time it's a dredge. I got to get a grip, got to sort out what to do. I've been a ghost for three years but now there's specters after me again.

Becky's curled up on the sofa, Jaz with her. Little kid's sleeping, sleeping good. Becky's got her eyes closed too but she's not sleeping. She's trying to block me out, block everything out. She's trying to forget.

Don't ask me how I know.

Only it won't work. Cos you don't forget. You don't ever forget. The specters come back wherever you go.

Can't make this troll out. She's not like Tammy and the rest. They're hard but she's beaten up, or beaten down, or both. She's certainly a dimpy mother. There's no way I'd leave a kid like Jaz with a crazy old dunny whose lights have gone out and who lets duffs off the street use her house for a drug den.

I wouldn't let Jaz out of my sight for two minutes if she was my kid.

But I'll tell you one thing about Becky—Trixi was wrong about her. The girl's not yellow. She's just scared and that's not the same thing at all. She's still got her eyes closed, see? But I'm telling you, she's wide-awake, and she's thinking hard.

Like I am.

Feels strange showing one of my snugs to someone. Haven't told her much about it. Guy who owns it works on an oil rig. One month on, one month off. I found out about him a couple of years ago and I've been keeping a check on where he is ever since. He won't be back here for another three weeks.

Got a lot going for it, this place. Old-fashioned lock, easy to pick. Ancient gobbo next door with a hearing problem. Empty flat on the other side. Only reason I don't come here more often is cos there's no books to read.

Becky's opened her eyes.

"You all right, Bex?"

She answers with a question.

"Where'd you learn to throw a knife like that?"

I was wondering when she'd bring this up. She's been carefully avoiding it all day.

"Doesn't matter where I learned it."

"Is that your way of telling me to mind my own business?"

"Maybe."

Silence. She's watching me hard now. Her eyes are blacker than ever with the lights on so low. She looks down at Jaz, still sleeping beside her, then back at me.

"Do that to my kid again and I'll kill you."

"I might just have saved her life. And yours."

"You could have killed her."

"But I didn't. And here we are. I've done everything I promised. I've found you a doss. I've given you some food."

"You call that food? Can of beans, can of mush, can of sweet corn?"

"I can't help it if the guy's got nothing else in the flat. He usually has some soup here."

She looks away. She's fizzing with pain, fizzing with anger. She pulls out a cig.

"Don't," I say.

She looks at me.

"No cigs, Bex."

"What the hell does it matter?"

"I don't leave traces in the snugs I use."

She stares at me, angrier than ever. I'm probably being stupid. Open the window and the smoke'll be gone by the time he gets back. But I'm so used to leaving nothing behind.

Maybe it doesn't matter. Maybe I'll just give up this snug, not use it anymore. Cos I'm starting to think something, Bigeyes. I'm starting to think this city's done for. They're here now. The specters are back. No place'll be safe anymore. All that I've built up here, all that I've learned from my hours of watching, counts for nothing.

I've got to start again.

Somewhere else.

Maybe they'll find me there too. But I've got to start again. And somehow I've got to hope.

Becky speaks again.

"I'll keep my promise."

I look at her.

"I'll be gone in the morning," she says. "Out of your life."

There's a long silence. Outside the flat I can hear cars pounding along the ring road. They're like distant voices, people I don't know going to places I don't know, speaking to no one.

My life's so dark now.

What happened to the light?

Remember that book I showed you last night? About a guy called Nietzsche? *Superman and the Will to Power.* There's something he says in it.

What doesn't destroy me makes me stronger.

Do you believe that, Bigeyes?

I don't know. I look at Becky and I don't know. I look at myself and I don't know. I look at you and I don't know. I don't even know if you're listening.

I don't feel stronger. I feel weak and small. I'm still here but I feel weak and small.

"Is that what you want?" says Becky.

I look back at her. She looks weak and small too. The only one here who looks strong is Jaz, lying there fast asleep.

"Is that what you want?" says Becky again. "Me and Jaz to go?"

I look at her. I look at Jaz. I hear myself speak.

"No."

22

DAWN. GUTTER GRAY. Rumble of cars still there. Haven't slept much. I turn on the radio. Been avoiding it but I got to know the worst.

"The news headlines. Police are hunting a girl of sixteen, named as Rebecca Jakes, and a boy of around fourteen, going by the nickname Slicky, in connection with the murder of a sixteen-year-old girl in the Carnside district of the city. The victim, whose name has not yet been made public, was found bludgeoned to death in a small—"

Becky switches it off.

"Don't want to hear that," she says.

"We need to know what they know."

"We already know what they know."

She looks over at Jaz. She's sitting in the corner, drawing another picture on the back of the one I messed up, ignoring the hole in the middle where the knife went through.

"Bex, we need to know what they're saying on the news."

She looks back at me, lowers her voice.

"The police were looking for me before I came here. But I met Trixi and the gang and went to ground at Tammy's gran's. I been keeping out of sight since then. But they'll know I'm here now. As for you . . ."

She runs her eye over me.

"You're a story in yourself."

"We need some breakfast."

"Don't change the subject."

"We still need some breakfast."

"Who are those men looking for you?"

"Never seen 'em before."

"But they know who you are. That man called you Blade. And he was right about that, wasn't he? You can't kid anyone about that now."

I give a shrug. But it doesn't shake her off that easily.

"So who are they?" she says.

"Just guys sent by other people."

"What other people?"

"I've made a few enemies."

"Like who?"

"Like it's time for breakfast."

I stand up, walk over to Jaz.

"Hey, Jaz!"

She looks up.

"What are you drawing?"

She shows me the picture. Another bird.

"That's nice," I say. "I promise not to mess it up this time. You hungry?"

She nods.

"I'll see what we got."

And there won't be much. The guy stocks up with cans of this and that but not much else. I head for the kitchen. Becky joins me and we hunt through the cupboards.

"There's some porridge oats," she says. "We could make that with some water. What else is there?"

"Some crackers." I'm hunting through another cupboard. "Bit of marmalade. Any margarine?"

She pulls open the fridge.

"Yeah." Takes the top off and sniffs it. "Seems okay."

We eat breakfast, wash up, stack away. Weird silence hanging over us. Guy next door's got his television on loud. Clatter at the door and a bundle of letters drops through to join the heap on the floor. Jaz goes back to her drawing. Becky and me sit at the table.

"We got to get away, Bex."

"I know," she says. "When?"

"Tonight. When it's good and dark."

"What we going to do today?"

"Stay here. Stay out of sight."

"The owner won't come back?"

"Not unless he's a good swimmer."

Silence. I look at her. She's like a little girl again, like Jaz almost. Only Jaz isn't scared.

"I'm scared too, Bex."

"I thought it was just me."

I shake my head.

And it's true, Bigeyes. I'm choked out. Cos I know it's all over. Everything's changed. I was free before. I was on top of my mountain, remember? And now the police want me, the gang wants me, and what's worse—the past wants me too. It's reaching out again like a corpse waking up.

Like it is for Becky.

She looks at me.

"Where are we going to go?"

"Away."

"Can't we hide in the city?"

"No."

"But you must know it really well."

"I know it better than anybody. That's why I know we've

got to go. There are too many people looking for us around here."

"So where can we go?"

"Don't know. Get away first and then decide."

She looks over her shoulder at Jaz. The little girl's frowning over her picture, like nothing else matters.

"Bex?"

She looks back at me.

"You got any money?" I say.

"No. You?"

"No. What about other stuff?"

"Couple of things back at Tammy's gran's house. Nothing I can't leave."

"Okay."

"We got to wait, then? Till tonight?"

"Yeah."

So we wait. Jaz draws, covers the paper, asks for more. Becky finds a pad of lined paper and another pencil and the two of them draw together. As for me, I think.

About all the things I've tried to forget—and for a moment it's like I'm seven years old again. I want to stand in the road like I used to and stop the traffic, and shout and swear and tell the whole world to go to hell. Only now it's all different. Cos this time they won't just watch. This time they'll run me down.

It's like my whole life's unraveled. I had it all tight like a little ball, but it was a ball of wool, and now someone's chucked it and the thing's rolling away, leaving the thread behind for all to follow.

Didn't take much to find me after all.

The gobbos and that hairy grunt must have been tracking

me for ages, must have seen me with the trolls on the towpath, or maybe just afterward heading for the bungalow. They certainly knew I was in there. It was me they were coming for when they smashed their way in.

And now Trixi's dead and probably Mary too.

How many more people are going to get rubbed out cos of me?

I'm looking at Becky, looking at Jaz, and I'm feeling choked again.

Day moves on like a slow dream.

And then evening comes.

We eat again, same meal as before. No one's speaking. It's like we're waiting for an execution. Television's still loud next door. Been on all day but I've hardly noticed it. We wash up, clear away, sit down again. Becky looks pale.

"Bex?"

"What?"

"Do you want to ring the police?"

"You kidding?"

"I don't mean to give yourself up. I mean to tell 'em about the guy who killed Trixi. And the other two who turned up. It'll give the police other people to look out for. Might even help you."

She shakes her head.

"I'm in enough trouble with the police as it is. There's no way they're going to believe anything I say. Anyway . . ."

She doesn't need to finish. I already know she's scared of the porkers.

I stand up.

"Come on, then. We got to go."

Becky stands up and holds out her hand to Jaz. The little girl takes it but looks up at me.

"You ready, Jaz?" I say.

She nods.

And then I remember something.

"Bex?"

"Yeah?"

"Take this, can you?"

I hold out the knife.

"I don't want it," she says.

"Neither do I."

"But you're the one who knows how to use it."

I know it too well, Bigeyes. That's the problem. I know the knife too well. Like I know the city too well. It's time to leave both behind.

"Take it, Bex. Please."

She takes it, puts it in her pocket.

"Thanks," I say.

I look around, check the flat, turn off the lights, open the door. All still. Corridor's dark and silent. Even next door's gone quiet.

We step out, wait, listen. Nothing moves, nothing murmurs. Just the sound of the traffic outside. Becky closes the door. Listen again, then down the stairs, soft and slow, floor by floor, and finally out and off into the night.

23

BLOOD SKY. STREETS DARK, houses dark, night dripping down. But the city's awake. She never sleeps, Bigeyes. She dozes but she never sleeps—and she sees too much.

Who else is watching, though?

That's the question.

There's enough people looking for us now. The police, the girl gang, all the others. I don't like to think about it. But the past has come back, hooked its claws into me. Life's dangerous again and I can't just think of myself like I used to.

Becky's walking funny, kind of a shuffle. Can't work out if she's tired or hurt. I know she's scared. She's not a fighting troll like Tammy and the others. She thought she was but she's not.

I can't make her out. It's not that I don't care about her. I do—a bit. But I can't crack her. We were getting on good back in the flat but hit the streets again and she chills up.

I don't need that right now. I need her to be strong. But she's turning into a millstone. It's like she's got no instinct for anything, not even looking after Jaz.

But I guess that's the real reason why I haven't blasted out of here. If it was just Becky, I'd tell her we got to split. But I can't walk out on Jaz too.

Look at her. Been living in a drug den and God knows

where else, got Becky for a mother, spends most of her time with dungpots and drifters and duffs off the street, or girls who'd stab you soon as blink, and here she is strolling through the night holding my hand like she's on her way to a party.

Like there's no danger. Like we got a place to go. Only we got no place to go.

Just the future. And what kind of a place is that?

No place for Jaz, I reckon. Not much of a place for me and Bex neither. Not for anyone with a past. And that's the thing, Bigeyes. To go to the future, you got to have a future.

I don't know if I got one. I got my past, same as Bex, whatever hers is, and then I got this—the effing present. Only it's no present you'd ever want. It's dark streets, dark houses, dark city, dark sky.

Becky's looking at me.

"Blade?"

"What?"

"How much farther?"

"Not far."

"What's that mean?"

"About five miles."

"That ain't far?"

I don't answer. She's only glumming cos I won't tell her where we're going.

She's right and she's wrong. About it being far, I mean. It's not far for her and me. When you got porkers and other nebs tramping on your shadow, five miles is a jink. We got to stuff it out of here quick as fly.

But she's right about Jaz.

Five miles for that little kid's going to hurt. Trouble is, I don't know what else to do. When we left the flat, I didn't have a clue where to take us. But then I had this idea.

Not a great one but it might help us on our way. So right now that's all I'm thinking of. That and how to get Jaz to where we got to go—and her dimpy mum.

"Keep going, Bex."

She glares at me. I take no notice, look at the kid instead.

"Jaz?"

She turns her head, fixes those eyes on me.

"Jaz? Do you want to ride on my shoulders?"

I'm half hoping she'll say no. She's light as breath but it won't take long for me to get tired if I go too far with her perched up there. She gives me this munchy smile.

I'm telling you, Bigeyes, she melts me, this kid. There's just something about her. She's like a pixie or an elf or something.

"Come on, then."

I hoist her up and she hooks her legs around my neck. I grab hold of her feet.

"You're getting heavier."

"No, I ain't."

She's got her arms around the top of my head. She pats me a couple of times on the scalp, funny little pats, like a baby petting a dog.

"Stop that."

I'm only joking but she stops. We walk on. I can feel Becky watching me. Hard to tell what she's thinking. Mixture of stuff probably. Glad to see me bonding with her kid, or maybe the opposite. But I can't be worrying about that now.

We got to walk. We got to get there. That's all that matters.

"Left here, Bex."

It's a narrow lane, no lights, no houses. She stops. I can see she doesn't want to go. She's just staring down it.

"What we got to go down there for?"

"Cos it takes us where we're going."

"And why won't you tell us where that is?"

"Cos it might not work out."

"You mean it's dangerous?"

Dangerous.

What kind of a stupid question's that, Bigeyes? I want to throttle this troll sometimes. It's like she thinks there's somewhere that's not dangerous for us. Like we can choose this road and not that one and everything'll be all right.

Only it won't. Cos every road, every path, every patch of ground's got danger for us now. And she knows that as well as I do. But I can't say all this with Jaz listening.

"Bex, I'm just saying it might not work out, okay?"

I lower my voice.

"Look, any way we go's risky right now. We're on the news. So we got to keep away from people and from CCTVs. We got to keep to lonely places. And this lane's a lonely place."

Some of the time. But I'm not telling her that.

"Where's it go?" she says.

"Through some playing fields. Then it splits up and one bit goes toward the city center. We'll take the other bit."

"Where's that go?"

"To the place I'm aiming for."

"The place you won't tell me about. The mystery destination."

Snarky voice but I'm not jiffed about that. I'm more bothered about shifting this troll. She's still blobbed there staring, like she's nailed to the ground.

Then suddenly she looks at me.

"Okay," she says.

And she sets off down the lane.

24

I FOLLOW, Jaz still perched on my shoulders. I know what you're thinking, Bigeyes. You're wondering why I won't tell Bex where we're going.

Well, you can go on wondering. I know what I'm doing. She's a loose bullet. I don't trust her to do things and I don't trust her to know things.

I don't trust you much either but that's another story.

Down the lane, on, on, darker down here than the streets we just left. This isn't a good place. Better than the streets, less exposed, but not a good place. I'll be happier when the playing fields open up. But that's not for a while yet.

High walls either side, see? There's a school behind that one. Wouldn't know it, would you? Waste ground behind the other one. You'll see it in a moment. I keep clear of this place normally.

Waste ground's got some funny nebs hanging around it—scavengers and druggies mostly, maybe the odd duff looking for something warm to sleep under. Dronky place but what choice have we got? Better among people who want to keep clear of the porkers like we do. They're less likely to give us away.

But we still got to watch ourselves. These nebs might hate the porkers but that doesn't mean they'll like us any better. Becky speaks, low voice.

"There's some people."

"I've seen 'em."

"Just ahead."

"I've seen 'em."

"Shall we turn back?"

"Keep walking."

Three figures, slumped against the wall. But they're muffins, no trouble at all. Don't ask me how I know.

"Blade?"

She's whispering now, and she's slowed down, more shuffly than ever. I whisper back.

"Keep moving. It's okay."

"But—"

"Keep moving. And shut up."

She does both, somehow. I can see she doesn't want to. She wants to scream her fear into the night sky, and turn and run. She's feeling in her pocket. I can see her hand fumbling about. She's searching for Trixi's flick knife.

"Bex."

I'm speaking dead soft. She looks around at me.

"Don't," I say.

She reads my face in spite of the darkness, pulls her hand out of her pocket.

No knife.

The figures are closer now—two men, dozy-looking gobbos, and a woman swigging from a bottle. They look up, take us in. I give Jaz's feet a little squeeze.

"Say hello to them, Jaz."

"Hello!" she calls out.

"All right, poppet?" says the woman.

We walk on. I give Jaz's feet another squeeze.

"Good girl."

She gives my head another one of those funny little pats. She's still light on my shoulders. I'm starting to think I could carry her forever.

On down the lane, wall on the right falling away. Waste ground opens up. We got to get past this bit quick. I'm hoping there's no trouble but you only need one claphead to start something.

So far, so good. Lane looks clear and nothing in the shadows to the right, nothing dangerous anyway. Just the big heaps of rubbish people dump here in the middle of the night, or whenever the coast looks clear.

"Something's moving," says Becky. "By the old fridge."

"It's a cat."

"You seen it?"

"I just said. It's a cat. There's another one farther off."

"Where?"

"Behind the pram."

I nod toward it. Becky looks.

"Can't see no cat."

"It's just gone."

She glances at me.

"You don't miss nothing, do you?"

I don't answer. I'm too busy missing nothing.

Another movement among the rubbish. Something low, a body under a blanket. A cough, twitch, wink of light as an eye opens. It fixes me for a moment, then closes again.

We walk on. Hum of the city over to the left. Night hum, like she's moaning, like she wants to rest but can't. I know this sound. I know all her sounds.

But this place is almost silent. Just a pattering among the rubbish, rats probably. Little squeal somewhere behind us, like the two cats just met. But it's soon quiet again. Then another sound.

Footsteps.

Stop, listen. Becky stops too, looks at me.

"What?" she says.

"Shh!"

Look around. No sign of anyone following, no more steps. Walk on. Sound starts again. Stop.

It stops.

I'm looking all around now, watching cute. Nothing moving on the waste ground, nothing on the lane.

"I didn't hear nothing," says Becky.

I feel Jaz playing with my hair like everything's okay. Walk on again, slow, steady. But I'm watching, listening, hard as I can. Can't see anybody, can't hear anybody. No more steps, just our own, and the hum of the city again farther off.

"I didn't hear nothing," says Becky again.

It's starting to rain, little feathery drops. Jaz gives a chuckle. I look up. Can't see her clear, just a bit of her face as she leans forward.

"Raining," she says, and she tugs my hair.

It's like everything's play to her, and for a brief, dimpy moment, I almost feel it too. But it doesn't last.

The footsteps are back.

Stop again, listen, look around. I can feel Becky watching me. I want to throttle her again. She should be watching the lane, the waste ground, not me. She should be checking for trouble.

"What?" she says.

I've seen him now, good way back down the lane, over by

the wall. Should have clapped him before. Either he's clever or I'm losing my touch.

He's stopped, keeping in the shadows. Can't make out his face but it's a gobbo, thick build. Watching me, that's for sure, even if I can't see his eyes.

"What?" says Becky again.

All she's got to do is look. Follow my gaze and look. But she's still watching me. I can feel it. She's just staring at me like a dimp.

"Over there." I nod down the lane. "In the shadows by the wall. A guy."

She says nothing but I feel her eyes lift off me.

"Can't see nobody," she says.

Jaz tugs at my hair again. I tickle her ankle, glance at Becky.

"Move on, slow. But keep your wits about you."

We move on down the lane. I don't look back. I'm not going to keep turning. I'll hear him now, even if he creeps after us. But he's not creeping. He's walking loud as you like. Knows we know and doesn't care.

I need to get some kind of a glimpse in case I know him. Not yet though. Got to act confident, like I don't care either.

Only I do. I don't like this stop-start stalking. Almost better if he just came on. But he's keeping his distance, watching but staying back.

Becky's all tensed up again. How she ever got in Trixi's gang's a blind-go for me. She must have done something, shown some bottle, or the trolls would never have let her in.

She's not showing much bottle now. She's choking out

again. I can see it. She's gone right down inside herself and she's not coming out.

"Bex."

I'm listening even as I speak, listening to the footsteps. They're still there, clear in the night in spite of the rain. And they're closer.

"Bex."

No answer, not even a glance. Now I look back, just quick, enough to see what I need to see. He's closer but still keeping to the shadows. I hear Becky stop.

I do the same, look at her. She's staring back down the lane.

She's got to see him now. He's stopped too and he's still in the shadows but he's much closer than last time she looked.

"Got him?" I say.

She sniffs, turns, walks on.

"Can't see nobody," she mutters.

She's lying, Bigeyes. I can always tell. And what's worse is she's zipping me over double-time. Cos you know what? There's something I feel as clear as the rain on my face.

She hasn't just seen that gobbo.

She knows who he is.

25

I'M SAYING NOTHING. I'm dead quiet. I'm watching around me, watching Becky. And I'm thinking: First question—if she knows him and doesn't want to tell me, what's she hiding?

Second question—how did he find us? Either it was luck or someone spotted us in the streets and told him. Doesn't matter who. Dregs know dregs. Word goes around, specially if there's money on the barrel.

Third question—if she knows him and doesn't want to go near him, does that mean he's dangerous? I can't make up my own mind about that. I usually know when I see people but I don't with this guy.

Fourth question—if he's dangerous, why's he hanging back?

Maybe he's just cautious, biding his time. Or maybe he's scared too. If he's heard about us on the news, there might be talk about how I'm useful with a knife, how I can throw 'em and stuff. Maybe they're saying this boy's lethal, keep away.

That could help us a bit. Or it could make things worse. Muffins keep their distance anyway. It's the nutters you got to watch, the hard nebs with something to prove.

Or the ones who don't care.

Becky's walking faster, not looking back, not looking at

me. Hard to know if she's scared of the gobbo or not. This is stupid. I might just as well ask her.

"Bex?"

"Don't ask me any questions."

Fair enough. Can't say I blame her. I've been telling her nothing. But Jaz speaks, in that little moony voice.

"Blade?"

First time she's used that name. Doesn't make me feel good to hear it. Not from her. Don't know why.

"What do you want, Jaz?"

"Want to get down."

"Okay."

I put her down. Feels strange without her up there. She was starting to get a bit heavy but it was nice carrying her. She takes Becky's hand. Becky looks at her, frowns a bit, like she doesn't want to be slowed down. Jaz takes no notice, just smiles. After a bit Becky smiles back at her.

"All right, Fairybell?"

Jaz nods.

I'm looking around again. Gobbo's still there but he's fallen back a bit. He's harder to see than he was but I'm sure he's speaking into a mobile. We've slowed right down now, or Becky has cos of Jaz. Maybe just as well. There's other things to watch for around here apart from the gobbo.

Waste ground's slipping away. Lane's narrowed and the playing fields are opening up on either side. And I'm starting to wonder, Bigeyes. I was going to take us straight on down the lane, then cut off right where it forks.

Now I'm not so sure.

Something about that gobbo's worrying me. He could be all kinds of trouble, specially if he's phoning people about us. He could be talking to the gang or the porkers. He might even be in touch with one of the ticks from my past. He could be one of their hired slugs.

I didn't think so at first but now I'm starting to wonder. God knows how many people they got working for them. There's the gobbo who killed Trixi, there's his mate, and there's that other guy, the big, hairy grunt. And now this new gobbo with his mobile.

He could be one of theirs too. Maybe I was wrong about Bex knowing him. Maybe she's got no idea who he is.

"He's called Riff," she says suddenly.

I look around at her. She's plodding along, still holding Jaz's hand, but she's watching me.

"That guy."

"I thought you said you couldn't see anybody."

"Well, I was lying. I saw him. And I know him."

I keep quiet. Best not to push her. She's dead tense. She'll tell me if I let her. Push her and she'll close up like a fist.

Rain's stopping but we're walking on through the night. Gobbo's a good way back now. Hasn't moved any farther. I can just make him out in the shadows. Think he's still talking on his mobile.

I look back at Becky. She's staring down at the ground, like she thinks she's said enough. I got to prompt her again. But Jaz speaks first.

"Riff," she says.

Becky glances down at her, then up at me.

"He's a mate of Tammy's gran's," she says. "Well, not a mate. More of a sponger."

I can guess. I remember Tammy's gran well enough. A right old dunny. Anyone could take her for a skydive.

A picture floats into my head of that other old lady—white-haired Mary with her scented candles and crazy dog. Nobody would ever call her a dunny. But I can't start drumming myself over that business again.

It hurts too much to think back. All I see is that bungalow. All I hear is the gunshots and the stabbing of my feet as I ran away and left her. There's no way she's still alive.

I got to break out of this, got to get back to what's cracking us now.

"Who's this Riff?" I say. "Apart from being a sponger."

"He's harmless. But he knows some scum."

"I bet he does."

But at least he won't know anyone from my past. Not if he's tied up with Tammy's gang. I suppose that's something.

"He hangs around with Trixi's brother," says Bex.

Trixi's brother? I never knew she had one. That's all I need to hear.

"Who's this brother?"

"He's called Dig."

"Older or younger?"

"Twenty."

"Mean as Trixi was?"

"You don't want to cross 'im."

"Turn left," I say.

"What?"

"Left. Cross the lane."

I feel her look at me, but I'm glancing back now. I need that Riff gobbo to see us. Trouble is, I can't see him. Don't tell me he's wigged it, Bigeyes. Hang on—I got him again. Still hanging back but he's there.

"Cross the lane, Bex. Move slow. We need that guy to see us."

She doesn't argue, just starts across the lane.

"Stop," I say.

She stops, Jaz still holding her hand. They're both looking at me. I bend down to Jaz, give her a smile.

"Riff," she says.

I don't see her mouth move in the darkness. All I see is those glowy eyes. It's like they're talking instead.

"Do you like him, Jaz?"

She says nothing, just stands there. I'm starting to feel something other than fear. I'm getting flashbacks again as I look into those bright little pools.

"Did he hurt you, Jaz? Did he do something you didn't like?"

I feel myself look away, down the lane to those quiet shadows, then back. Jaz is still watching me, like she's been waiting to answer. She shakes her head.

"Riff's harmless," says Becky. Her voice sounds harsh in the night. I'd almost forgotten she's there. I straighten up, glance back down the lane again.

"Let's hope he's seen us crossing the lane."

"What for?" says Becky.

"Never mind. Come on."

I lead them right across to the fence. It's an easy climb into the playing field beyond and Jaz is small enough to crawl through the little gap in the wire.

"Go through there, Jaz. It'll be fun."

She doesn't hesitate, just crawls through. I'm over the top by the time she's in the field, Becky just behind.

"Now what?" she says.

"We want to make it look to that Riff guy like we're running across this field."

"What for?"

"So he can tell that to his mates on his mobile. But we'll cut back farther down to the lane, cross it where he can't see us, and lose 'im over the fields on the other side."

But already I can see that's not going to work.

There's lights moving toward us from both ends of the lane.

26

DIFFERENT KINDS OF LIGHTS. Car headlights behind us, some way back. But it's the lights coming from the other direction that bother me more.

They're flashlights, and there's lots of 'em.

They're also some way down but if we'd hung about another minute, one or other of these nebs would have seen us. Trouble is, we're going to have problems cutting over the lane farther down with these flashlight carriers trigging up.

"Come on," I say. "We got to move fast."

I pick Jaz up and set off.

"Want to walk," she says.

"Got to carry you, baby, okay? I'll put you down soon as I can. Promise."

She doesn't argue. Thank God she's a sweet kid.

We're running now. Becky keeps up easy with me carrying Jaz. I'm trying to think as we run. There's still a chance we can double back farther down but we got to make sure we're over this field and well out of sight of the lane before we cut right.

And we got to cut right. We can't go into the city again. To get to where I want to take us, we got to go in the same direction as the lane. If we give these nebs a wide enough berth, we could still manage it as long as we keep 'em off our scent when they come looking this way.

Cos that's what they're going to do. I know it.

We're halfway over the playing field. Rugby posts, changing rooms, pavilion. We run past, but I'm getting tired now. Look back.

Headlights by the fence along the lane, figures standing there. It's porkers—two cars, four nebs, no dogs.

But the flashlights have gone.

Switched off anyway. They don't want to see the porkers any more than we do. Question is, where are these other nebs? They haven't cut into this field. We're almost on the far side but I'd have seen 'em easy.

And now I'm getting a new pile of thoughts.

Risky thoughts, Bigeyes. Scary too. But they won't let me go. I'm thinking, I got to know more about those flashlights. They're after us, that's for sure, but who are they?

Not just the three gobbos who were hunting me before. I know that much. I saw at least five lights on the lane. I got to know who these people are. I got to know what they look like, how dangerous they are.

Yeah, yeah, I know about Bex and Jaz. I know I got to get 'em away. But I got to know who's after us too. I got to know my enemies.

"What's up?" says Becky.

She's looking at me as we run.

"You got something on your mind," she says. "I can see it in your face."

"Tell you in a minute. Let's get clear first."

We run on. Still no sign of anyone in the field behind us. I got no idea where the flashlights are now but hopefully they haven't spotted us either. The porkers are where they were before. I can see the lights from their cars burning up the night.

Jaz is getting heavy but we've reached the far end of the playing field. Stop by the wall, breathing hard.

"Down," says Jaz.

"I know, baby." I put her down. "There you go."

"What now?" says Becky.

"You and Jaz are going to hide behind this wall. There's a way over farther down where the brickwork's collapsed a bit."

"How do you know?"

"I just do. Climb over—it's dead easy—and keep out of sight. There's some bushes on the other side and a little patch of scrubby ground."

"And what are you going to do?"

"Go back."

"What for?"

"To check those people out."

"But we got to get away. You said we got five miles to go to this place of yours. What's it matter who's after us? We know it's people we don't want to see. That's enough for me. It's like one in the morning or whatever and I just want to get the hell out of here."

I'm looking at her. She's right. We should wig it out of here, for Jaz's sake if nothing else. But it's no good, Bigeyes.

I got to get a closer look at these nebs. I might not recognize any of 'em. They might just be hired slugs. But I got to know what kind of shit's after us.

"Stay here," I tell Becky. "And stay quiet. I won't be long."

She doesn't answer, just scowls. Jaz looks up, like she's waiting for something.

"She wants a kiss," says Becky.

I hear the threat in her voice.

I look down at Jaz. Long time since I kissed anyone. Last person was Becky—not this Becky, the other Becky. The ever-special Becky. The dead Becky. But I don't want to talk about that now.

I lean down, give Jaz a kiss on the cheek. Feels kind of weird.

"Bye," she says, and she turns to Becky like I'm not there anymore.

Like I've never been there.

"Jaz? You all right, kid?"

"She thinks you're never coming back," says Becky.

"What?"

"She's used to people not coming back. That's why she wanted a kiss from you. She thinks you're leaving us for good."

"Bex—"

"And maybe you are." Becky looks at me hard. "Maybe this is it. You don't want us around your neck. You can move better on your own. We're just a nuisance."

I glance down at Jaz again. She's clutching Becky's leg, pushing her face into the thigh. She's not crying or anything. She's just . . . I don't know . . .

"She's trying to forget you," says Becky.

I bend down, stroke Jaz's hair. She doesn't move, doesn't look around. Feels strange doing this. I don't like being close to people normally. But it's okay with her.

"Jaz," I whisper. "I'm only going away for a few minutes. I'll be back. I promise I'll be back."

She doesn't turn around, just goes on pressing her face into Becky's thigh.

"Jaz?"

She moves her head, just enough for me to see her right eye. It's got tears in it.

I'm losing it now, Bigeyes. I can't cope with this. I'm thinking, maybe I should just stick here, get us away, forget those nebs.

But it's no good. No matter how much this kid burns me up, I got to know what's out there.

I give her another kiss on the cheek. She doesn't move, doesn't speak.

"I'll be back, Jaz. Promise I will."

She says nothing, just looks at me with that wet little eye. I feel something drop into my pocket. I know what it is without looking. I glance back at Becky.

"I don't want the knife."

"Keep it," she says. "You're more likely to need it than me. And you know how to use it."

I reach into my pocket, squeeze the knife, hold it tight.

"Keep it," she says.

I let go, pull my hand out. The knife feels heavy in my pocket, heavier than it should. I don't know why.

"I'll see you," I say.

And I'm gone.

27

GOT TO THINK. Got to get back to being me, being strong, being alone. Got to forget about Bex and Jaz for a few minutes. If I'm worrying about them, I'll get snagged.

Check over my shoulder. Becky's found the broken-down section of the wall and she's helping Jaz over it. Least she's doing what she's supposed to. I just hope she waits there till I get back.

Okay, got to wipe 'em out of my mind. Got to play stealth.

Still no one in the field, no one I can see anyway. I'm moving low, moving slow, listening hard, thinking cute. I need to head for where the flashlights were. I know the nebs are still around. I can feel 'em.

The porkers haven't gone either. Their cars are still there, lights on, and I can see two figures in the lane. Cut left, over the hockey field.

Stop, look about, listen.

Move on, creep through the bushes, into the next hockey field, stop again. Lane's closer now, over to the right. I can see it clearly and even the playing fields on the other side.

I was right not to bring Bex and Jaz here. There's people in this field. Can't see 'em but I can sense 'em. I'm crouched low. I'm like a cat. I'm moving small but ready to spring. I can't run fast, so I need all the head start I can get if they come for me.

Trouble is, where are they?

Got 'em.

Far side of the field, where the fence down the opposite end meets the lane. Little group of figures, close together, flashlights off. They must have climbed over and cut back here the moment they saw the headlights coming.

Don't think the porkers have spotted 'em. Probably didn't even see the flashlights. Hard to tell how many nebs there are in the darkness.

I'm trying to work out how to get close. Best to climb over the fence on the far side of the field, then sneak down behind it.

Let's go.

Rain's starting again, soft like before. Feels good on my face. I'm moving slow still, watching the figures all the time. They're quiet. Can't hear any voices. Like they're waiting. For the police maybe.

Or me.

Don't think they've seen me. I'm so low to the ground and I'm keeping well to the left. Now I can hear voices, a deep murmur.

Then silence again.

Sound of an engine revving up behind me. Headlights flashing over the lane. The porkers are leaving. First car's turning in the lane, now the second.

I've stopped. I'm watching 'em drive back toward the spot where that Riff guy was standing. And I'm wondering where he is now. Cos things are getting confusing, Bigeyes.

Someone's tipped off the porkers about us. Don't ask me how I know. Someone's seen us trigging through the streets and recognized us from the news reports and blotched on us.

It won't be those duffs we saw. They won't want anything to do with the police. And it won't be Riff. He wants us for the gang. It's probably some curtain twitcher.

But then there's these other gobbos. Someone's shunted us with them too. They didn't get here by chance.

I got to find out all I can.

I'm moving again, low, slow. More voices from the figures, louder, more confident now that the porkers have gone. But they're still sitting there, in no hurry to blast off.

Here's the fence. Stop, listen. Gobbos down to my right now, half hidden by shadow. They're in a dip too, kind of a shallow ditch with just their heads and shoulders showing. One of 'em's moving.

Freeze.

He's twisting around. I'm like stone. I'm holding breath, dead still. They've gone silent. No one's talking.

More heads turning. Eyes shifting toward me. I can't see the glints but I can feel 'em splitting the dark, splitting my space. They can't see me. I keep telling myself they can't see me. I'm good at being invisible. That's how I survive.

Only why haven't the heads turned back again? Why are they still staring toward me? I'm low, I'm in the shadow, I'm still, I'm quiet. Why are they looking?

That's when I hear it.

The pad of footsteps coming up behind me.

Shit, Bigeyes. I'm in the grime. I flick my head around.

There he is, sneaking up—and I know him. It's the gobbo

who killed Trixi. Tense up, fix him, get ready to spring, left or right. Can't fight him. It's run and run.

Only not yet. Wait till he lunges.

But he doesn't. It's only when he's almost on me that I realize he hasn't seen me. He's watching the gobbos and they're watching him. That's why they turned to look.

But he's still going to see me any moment, unless I keep dead still and he keeps not looking. One of the gobbos calls out.

"Took your time, Paddy," and a moment later the guy's past me and with his mates.

Paddy.

So that's his name. Another little detail to add to the picture. Paddy—smooth talker, smooth looker, age about thirty, scumbo, murderer, hired slug.

Sent to bring me back.

Only I'm not going back. Not to where they come from. I'd rather die first.

I'll tell you something, Bigeyes. There's bad places and there's shit places, and then there's hell. And I've been in all three.

I'm not going back.

I'm looking for the other two, the gobbo who was with him before and the hairy grunt. Trouble is, I can't see these guys clear in the darkness. If Paddy's after me, then the other two must be as well. I got to get closer, got to see 'em clearer, got to hear what they're saying.

I just hope they don't switch their flashlights back on too soon.

They're talking again, low voices, too quiet to pick out any words. Creep left, not too fast but not too slow either. I got to hear 'em before they split. They could go any moment. And I got to stay hidden.

Here's the other fence. Over or under? I'm looking for a way under. It's safer.

No good. Gap's too small. Check right. Hard to see much now. There's a bush in the way. But that's going to help me too.

Over the fence, dead slow, slither down the other side. No sound of movement from the gobbos, just the same murmur of voices.

Creep on, other side of the fence. I'm close now. I can see the ditch running along the line of the fence. And there's the first of the gobbos.

Stop, stiffen, watch. Inch to the left, just a fraction. I'm lying on my front now, peering through the gap along the bottom of the fence. And there below me in the ditch are six men.

I can see their faces now in spite of the darkness. Three of 'em I recognize straight up—Paddy, his mate, and the big grunt. The other three are strangers but they're tough-looking gobbos. If they're looking for me too, then I'm in even bigger grime than I thought I was.

Paddy speaks.

"So nobody's seen the boy?"

I see a shaking of heads.

"We was stuck here," says the grunt, "while you was off with Riff."

Riff!

These guys know Riff! Shit, Bigeyes. I wasn't expecting that. And if they know Riff, then they got to know the gang as well, and Trixi's brother. They must have made contact some way. Don't ask me how.

But I'll tell you one thing. They won't have told Tammy that Paddy killed Trixi. They'll have said it was me or Bex. Maybe that's why they're working together. More eyes for the hunt.

But the gobbos are playing a game of their own.

The grunt goes on.

"We couldn't move cos o' the police." He pauses. "What you done with the other two?"

The other two? I feel a shudder, a hot mist of fear. Paddy answers.

"I let Riff take the little kid."

I give a start. It can't be right. Not Jaz. It's got to be someone else.

"And the girl?" says the grunt.

I don't want to listen, don't dare to listen. But it's too late now. Paddy's speaking again. And his words chip open my heart.

"I killed her."

28

I FEEL THIS PAIN like I've been stabbed.

I didn't know that was possible. I thought I was dead to caring. But I've been opened up again. Jaz and Becky have walked into my life and now the kid's taken and Becky's dead. And it's my fault. What have I done?

The men are arguing.

"Jesus, Paddy!"

"That was stupid!"

"What you done that for?"

"I had to," he says. "She might have talked."

"But we was told to keep a clean slate. Just go for the boy."

"I couldn't help it," says Paddy. "All right?"

"Like you couldn't help it in the bungalow. And now you done two."

There's an angry murmur from the others.

"I've hidden the body," says Paddy. "They won't find her for a bit."

They fall silent, like they need to think.

I'm desperate to get out of here. Got to find out what that gobbo's done. It won't be easy. There's loads of places he could have hidden her. Ditches, bushes, refuse tips. But I got to try.

Only I can't just run. I still got to think and creep and play stealth or they'll see me. I can't bear this, Bigeyes. I'm being ripped apart. I'm lying here inches from the nebs who've come to find me and take me back, and the guy who killed Becky, and I'm trying to think, trying to stay calm. But every bit of me's out of control.

Breathe, make yourself breathe.

I breathe, as slow and quiet as I can, only it's juddery and raspy and loaded with the tears I'm trying to hold back. One of the gobbos turns, looks my way.

I can see his eyes, clear as pain. They're bright and dangerous. Can he see me? I don't know. I close my eyes in case he catches the glint. No sound from the gobbos, not even talking.

What are they doing? What's that guy doing? I haven't heard him move, can't feel him coming near. I want to open my eyes but I don't dare. I'm screwing them up tight in case he sees them. I can feel the tears drowning them, drowning me.

I open my eyes and there's the gobbo still watching. He's got to have seen me. Surely he's got to have seen me? Then he turns, lights a cig, and says, "Let's go."

The others don't move. I'm watching 'em through blurred eyes. I'm taking 'em in, trying to forget the pain and do what I know I got to do. I'm looking at the faces, fixing 'em in my mind, remembering.

Cos this is where it all changes. This is where I stop being prey.

The grunt's standing up. He looks down at the guy with the cig.

"Lenny's right," he says. "We won't find him sitting around. Let's go."

Lenny—another name. I fix him in my mind, fix and remember. How quickly hate has come back. I thought I'd left it behind but I was wrong.

They're all standing up. Paddy reaches out, takes Lenny's cig, lights one of his own from the tip, hands the cig back. Then he looks around at the others.

"Come on," he says, and they climb out of the ditch and head for the lane. A moment later, they're gone—and I'm over the fence and racing across the hockey field.

I'm still crying, Bigeyes, crying as I run. I should be looking around me, checking for trouble in case those gobbos have tricked me and knew I was there all the time and have cut back from the lane to catch me—but I can't.

I can't even care about that. I'm racing blind, blubbing and screaming and torn up with anger and hurt and fear. I'm over the hockey field, over the next, stumbling through the dark and the rain, and here's the broken-down wall, and I'm over.

And they're not there.

How could they be? Every part of me knew they wouldn't be. But every part was hoping I was wrong, hoping I hadn't heard right, hoping Paddy was zipping his mates over to impress them.

Only he wasn't. He was telling the truth. And I knew it all along.

There's no point looking for Bex. She's dead and she's gone and it's my fault. I kneel down on the spot where they last were.

"Bex."

I'm talking to a shadow but I can't stop myself.

"Bex, I'm sorry. Please . . . I'm sorry."

I'm staring about me through the tears, trying to work out

what happened. There's a stick nearby, a big, heavy thing. Maybe it was that. It would have done the job. One blow would be enough.

I don't want to think about what Jaz saw.

"I'm sorry, Bex."

I shouldn't have left her. I shouldn't have left Jaz.

"I'm sorry, I'm sorry."

I shouldn't have gone. I should have taken 'em away from here, kept 'em safe.

I stand up, look around, try to think. Rain's still falling. Wind's picking up. Sky's darker than ever. I'm standing here in the early hours of the morning and I know this is the moment.

I'm on my own again like I was before. I can do what I planned to do with Bex and Jaz. I can wig it out of here, make my escape. Or I can do the other thing.

Turn hunter.

I don't have to think. I knew the answer the moment Paddy smirked his news. I pull out the knife, flick it open. The blade moistens with rain like it's shedding tears.

"Listen . . ."

I'm speaking low. I don't know who to. Who am I speaking to, Bigeyes?

I squeeze the knife and understand.

I'm speaking to Becky—the Becky who just got killed, and the old Becky, the Becky who knew me, the Becky who died too. And I know they're listening.

I look down at the knife. I can see both Beckys clear, bright in the blade. I close it up, folding the tears inside the hilt. And I speak to them again.

"This is for you."

29

I'M RUNNING AGAIN, back to the lane, and down it. Not the way we came. The way we were going, the way the gobbos are going. I can't see 'em. They're some way ahead. If they haven't cut off somewhere, I'll see 'em in a few minutes, as long as they aren't running too.

And why should they? What have they got to be scared of here? Certainly not a kid like me.

But that's where they're wrong. This isn't their patch. It's mine. My city. They don't know her like I do. And they don't know me, not like they think they do.

On, on, running hard, rain still falling. That's the only moisture left on my face. My tears are on the inside now, and I want 'em to go on flowing. I don't want 'em to stop. I don't want 'em ever to stop.

I'm moving fast now, even though I'm tired. I need to slow down. I'm worried in case my brain stops when I see 'em. If I let anger take over, I won't win. Not with six of 'em. I got to make myself think, plan, watch.

Stop! I've seen 'em—a large, moving shadow far down the lane. They're keeping together, moving quiet, still no flashlights on. They must have thought I was close when they had 'em on before.

I still can't believe they made contact with Riff and the trolls. I wonder what story Paddy told to make 'em think Becky or I killed Trixi.

But what does it matter? I know who my enemies are. And here's six of 'em walking ahead of me.

No one's looked back. Move to the side of the lane, keep in the shadow, slink and follow. Play stealth. I'm calming down now, turning cool like I need to, but I'm breathing blood.

I'm so dangerous it scares me.

But this isn't the time to act. Keep back, watch, follow. I'm gripping the knife in my pocket. I'm squeezing it. I want to pull it out, flick it open. Memories are flooding me, pictures from the past I don't want to see. But I can't stop 'em. They're filling me up like liquid pain, they're mixing with the tears and the anger and the hate, and the guilt.

That more than anything.

I'm looking at the backs of those gobbos and I'm folding up inside. Cos it's not just the pictures of the past that are coming back. It's the pictures of Jaz being carried away, it's the pictures of Becky lying somewhere dead. Her body must be cold now, cold and wet and growing hard.

And I put her in that place. I left her to die.

I squeeze the knife again.

Don't look at me like that, Bigeyes. Just don't. Don't look at me at all. You don't understand. It's about revenge now. But I got to do it my way.

They're slowing down. The grunt's at the back and he's getting tired. He's strong but he's not fit. Not surprised with all that beef and gut. The others are looking around at him. He's stopped now, catching his breath.

They all stop. Paddy's lighting another cig. They're muttering something.

Freeze!

One's looking back down the lane. Steal closer to the fence, crouch down low. A light flashes on, one of the flashlights, flicks about, searching. I keep still, keep low. If they come for me, I'll have to blast out quick.

No good wigging it back up the lane. They'll catch me even with this head start. Best to scramble over the fence and make for the railway line. Easier to lose 'em around there.

But they don't come for me. Flashlight goes off, and the gobbos move on.

I slip after 'em, slow, slow, close to the fence. I'm deep in shadow and I'm watching their backs, watching for the first to turn around. But they're pushing on, even the grunt, though he's blowing like a gale.

Now I got to watch it. There's more duffs coming into view. Couple just ahead, close to the fence. The gobbos haven't even glanced at 'em but if either of 'em talks to me, it could be hard. The gobbos could hear.

Stop, wait, let the gobbos get ahead. Move on again. Just as well I waited. First duff pipes up straightaway.

"Got yourself lost, kid?"

I don't answer, walk on. I'm nearly past when his mate jumps up.

I've got the knife out before he can blink. It's open and bright and hissing around his face. He steps back, his eyes on the blade.

I hold it still, watching him. I can feel the other duff slumped close by. His mate's still watching the knife, then he shrugs and says, "Yeah, well," and sits down again.

I close the knife, put it back in my pocket, move on.

Now's the danger time. Not before when he was facing me. They're both muffins. They can't hurt me. But now they can cause trouble. They can shout abuse. They can make the gobbos turn around to look.

But neither of the duffs calls out.

The gobbos are some way ahead now. Walk on, still keeping back, but I got to keep 'em in sight, got to see which way they go. Right now it's straight on down the lane but they're getting close to the fork where it branches off toward the city or away around the outskirts.

Where I was taking Bex and Jaz. My escape plan. It wasn't bad either. I could still use it if I wanted. But it's no good thinking about it.

Everything's changed now. The past and the present have joined up again.

More duffs ahead, but they're even less trouble than the last two, all of 'em lying by the side of the lane, sleeping or dozing or drugged out. They probably don't even know I'm here.

Walk past, eyes back on the gobbos, another quarter of a mile, and another, and then a mile, and I'm still watching 'em. Why didn't they drive this way? They didn't have to walk up the lane. But I think I get it.

No headlights, no warning. Somebody saw us and tipped 'em off—Riff probably—and they came to meet us, maybe spread out at first with flashlights, keeping in touch by mobile.

Best that way. Then if the porkers show up like they did, they can split and hide and regroup later.

And there's another thing—they never intended to take

Bex and Jaz. If they'd wanted to capture us all, they'd have brought whatever they're driving up the lane. Too much fuss to carry all three of us, especially if we made any noise.

I'm guessing that's why Paddy rubbed out Bex and let Riff have Jaz. He just wants me. Well, he hasn't got me yet.

But here's the fork and there's a van parked on the verge.

The gobbos have stopped.

Freeze, wait, watch 'em cute. I'm still safe in the shadow. They're talking, low voices. Grunt's still wheezing but he's taken a cig from Paddy and he's lighting up.

Rain's stopped.

Creep closer. There's lots I can do but it's all dangerous. Simplest stuff first. License plate. Can't make it out. Got to get nearer.

Creep, creep, low, low. I'm hearing the city again. She's over to the left. She's been talking all this time, like she always does, only I haven't been listening. I haven't been able to listen. I've had to keep my wits trimmed on these dregs.

And I'm still doing that, more than ever.

So why'm I hearing the city again? Tell me, Bigeyes. Why'm I hearing her again? A low murmur, like she's not happy cos she can't sleep, like she knows she never will. Or maybe it's just that she's seen too much, too much of nebs like me and them.

Too much of what's going to happen next.

30

THE GRUNT GIVES A COUGH, brings my mind back.

License plate. I can read it now. Run over it a couple of times in my mind—done. I'm quick remembering, like I remember all the stories I've read.

Now I'm taking in the other stuff. The van, the gobbos, the fork in the lane, the rubbish dumped over the fences, the fields stretching away beyond—and then the van again.

I've got ideas flooding my mind but there's only one I care about. It's so strong I can't let it go. Don't try and talk me out of it, Bigeyes.

It's too late for words now. I've got both Beckys in my mind. I'm seeing 'em clear, I'm seeing Jaz, I'm seeing all the other stuff. I'm breathing blood so bad I want to rip up the sky.

Creep closer, through the gap in the fence, down the other side. Gobbos on my right, far side of the lane, lounging, smoking, murmuring. Two of 'em having a pee. Paddy's talking on a mobile.

A rat scudders past me, disappears in the bushes. I'm close to the rubbish on this side of the lane now. It's not so big a tip as the waste ground we passed earlier but there's plenty of stuff for what I need.

Another rat. Stops, looks at me, disappears like the last

one. Move on, watching the shadows of the men beyond the fence, but I'm searching too, searching the piles of junk.

I soon find what I want. Shove it under a bush, move on, quiet, slow, picking up stones. Stop at the fence, peer through.

They're still there but they've stopped talking, apart from Paddy on his mobile. They're restless—I can tell—like they want him to hurry up. They keep turning and looking at him.

I'm watching him too, Bigeyes.

You bet I am.

He's finishing his call. He gives a smug little chuckle like everything's okay with the world, like he's never hurt a fly in his life, puts the mobile in his pocket, turns to the others. They're watching him close now.

But not as close as me.

I choose one of the stones, watch, wait. He nods 'em toward the van and they start to move. I throw the stone into the darkness, well over their heads.

There's a soft thud among the rubbish on the other side of the lane.

The gobbos stop.

Not a word from any of 'em but they're staring over the rubbish where the stone landed. One of 'em speaks at last, low voice. But I catch it.

"Probably a cat."

He doesn't sound convinced.

I wait, watch. They're still staring toward the rubbish beyond the lane, like they're waiting for another sound. Paddy nods toward the van again.

"Let's go. It won't be him."

A laugh from the other gobbos, a strained kind of laugh. And I'm thinking, yeah—laugh away, laugh your faces off. It won't be the boy. This is the last place he'll be right now.

Laugh away.

I throw another stone, over to the left.

They stiffen, all at once. Now they're really looking, all directions this time. They're not stupid. Even the grunt's looking all around him.

But they don't see me. I'm in a little dip now, just behind the bottom level of the fence. There's garbage bags and old tin cans for company but I don't care about that. I can see 'em clear but I'm out of sight for when the flashlights come on.

And there we go. Six lights flash out.

I dip my head a bit more, just to be safe. But I'm still watching. I'm watching like only I know how to watch. They're still grouped together and they're nervous. I can see it from the way they're standing.

Six big guys and they're scared of an unknown noise.

I could tell 'em about being scared. I could tell 'em about the unknown.

I take another stone. Got to be careful this time. With the flashlights on they might catch sight of it flying through the air. I wait, watch—and throw, well beyond 'em, deeper among the rubbish on the other side.

The gobbos turn that way.

"Come on," says Paddy.

And they're over the other fence, all six of 'em, blundering through the rubbish. The moment they're out of sight, I'm over my fence and by the van, knife open. Two tires'll do. No, make it three. Shit, make it four. Why not?

Zap! Then a sweet hiss.

Three more, then back over my fence and into the dip again. I'm breathing hard but I quiet myself, close the blade, put the knife back in my pocket, check the lane again.

Here they come, one by one, climbing back over the other fence. The grunt's last. He looks bombed out. The others are already by the van, waiting for him.

And I'm waiting for them.

Cos I haven't finished yet. But first someone's got to see what's happened. The grunt does it for me.

"The tires," he says.

They look around at him, then down at the wheels.

"Shit!" says one.

They go all the way around the van, muttering, swearing. But I'm watching Paddy's face. He hasn't said a word, hasn't shown a flicker of anger.

He's looking around him again, checking the lane with his flashlight.

"Spread out," he says.

Yeah, good move, Paddy. Get 'em to spread out.

Only not you.

I need you here.

They're moving about the lane, slowly, flashing their beams this way and that. I keep low.

Come on, Paddy. I need you over here.

He's stopped, middle of the lane. Three of the gobbos have climbed back over the fence again to search the rubbish on the other side. The grunt and another guy have wandered off, checking the verges.

Paddy's still standing close to the van.

Come on, Paddy. I need you over here.

He speaks, not loud, like he knows he doesn't need to.

"She didn't put up much of a fight."

He's staring toward my side of the lane. He can't see me. But he might as well be looking right into my face. Cos his words are going right to my heart. As he knows they are.

"You'll find her in a ditch." He gives a mocking little laugh. "If you want to bother looking, that is. I wouldn't waste my time if I were you. Life's short. Don't you agree?"

Yeah, Paddy. I agree.

I can see the other flashlights stabbing the night. But they're no danger. They're in another world. There's only two people in my world right now.

Me and Paddy.

He's looking in my direction, looking hard, and I'm wondering, Bigeyes—is this fate? Or is it me? Can I pull him here by mind alone?

Like that book I showed you.

The Will to Power.

Yeah, the will to power.

Only now it's different. I'm looking at you, Paddy, and I'm asking you—who's got the power now? Who's got the will?

He's still looking this way.

"Come on." I'm whispering to him. "Come on."

He comes on, slow, unsure of himself, flicking the beam of his flashlight right and left. It falls over the rubbish piles behind me, falls over me even, but I'm still too low for him to see me.

He's close to the fence now.

I slip down to the right, keeping in the dip. The flashlight goes on searching, but it's missing me altogether. On the far side of the lane I hear the gobbos throwing rubbish about as they search the ground.

"Come on," I whisper.

Paddy climbs over the fence. All I see of him now is the glare of the flashlight and beyond that a ghost of what he was. What does he see of me?

Nothing.

Cos I'm a ghost too. I'm doing what I do best. It's as easy as lifting wallets.

Only this time I'm lifting a man's life.

What'll he see in those last few seconds? Is it like they say? Everything flashing before you as you die? All the things you've done? Or is it just the snuffing of a light, like switching off his flashlight?

He doesn't see me move, doesn't see me reach under the bush for the cricket bat, doesn't see me at all till I'm right in front of him. Cos I'm not doing it from behind, Bigeyes. I'm doing this right.

He stiffens, opens his mouth.

No words come out. The blow to his stomach has smashed away his breath. Another to the chin, another to the back of the head. He gives a gasp, totters. I knock the flashlight out of his hands, kick his legs away.

He falls down as far as his knees but he's still upright. He fumbles with his hands but he's dazed, he's not moving right, he's got no guard up at all. He's looking at me, his face as twisted as his heart, and he's mouthing something. Cos he knows what's coming.

Only I don't care to hear.

I look into his eyes. All I see in them is the blood I've come to spill. I speak. I don't recognize my voice.

"This isn't for Becky. It's for me."

He doesn't answer. He just stares. He knows it's all over. I drop the bat, pull out the knife, flick it open.

Kiss the blade.

31

Dawn. Light without light. November sun creeping over the city. But it's dragging darkness with it, like the day's working in reverse. I'm alone, I'm safe, I'm out of sight.

But I'm eating myself alive.

Or dead.

What's the difference? Maybe there is no difference. Life or death, heads or tails. Spin a coin, make your call.

I had to rub him out, Bigeyes. It was revenge. It was right. I had to kill him. Are you listening? I had to kill him.

So why didn't I?

Why's he still alive?

Tell me.

I keep looking at the knife, keep flicking it open, closing it, flicking it open. What happened? I got pictures in my head but they're dronky pictures, like the ones Jaz draws. They don't make sense.

I got a picture of Paddy's face, his eyes watching me, his mouth pleading. No words, nothing like that, just his lips moving, begging, and then another picture—of me turning.

Running.

It can't be right. I don't do that. I've never done that, not when it's the business. I'm Blade. I'm called that for a reason. I don't mess up. I'm Blade. I'm bloody stinking effing Blade.

Only I didn't kill him. I turned and ran.

Help me, Bigeyes. I don't know what I am.

More sun, more darkness. Everything's inside out, everything's not what it should be. Put the knife in my pocket, look about me . . .

An alleyway, Bickton estate. How'd I get here? Can't remember. Hang on, stuff's coming back. I chose this place for a reason. What was it? Must have had a reason.

Outskirts of the city, that's it. Outskirts of the city, outskirts of the outskirts. Sleepy houses, sleepy nebs. That's got to be reason number one—nobody watching. What's reason number two?

Think. Make yourself think.

What's reason number two? There's got to be one. It can't just be that the place is sleepy.

Phone booth.

That's it—phone booth. Got to make that call. Should have done it hours ago, only I haven't been thinking. I've just been drummed out of my brain, slumped here catching shadows in my head. Not doing the stuff I should be doing.

THINK!

Forget about Paddy. Forget about the knife. Forget about what you didn't do. Get your head cranked.

"Phone booth."

That's it. Talk aloud.

"Phone booth. Make the call."

I'm on my feet, peering out the alleyway. All snoozy on the estate but we still got to be careful, Bigeyes. There's plenty of nebs around here with radios and television sets, plenty who'll know about the boy the porkers are looking for.

So far, so good. Curtains drawn across the windows. All

quiet, just the hum of the city farther off—and right now I'm glad to hear her. Over the road to the phone booth. Check there's a tone—good. Think, breathe, think, breathe.

What kind of accent? I'm best at Scottish.

Nine, one, one.

A man answers. I ask for the police. He puts me through. A woman comes on.

"Police emergency services, can I help you?"

Shit, she's Scottish.

"Can I help you?" she says again.

I'll try Irish.

"I've got some information."

Doesn't sound very Irish but it's the best I can do.

"Okay," she says. "But could I just take your name and phone number?"

"No, you can shut up and listen. I've got some information and you can have it for free. But if you start buzzing questions at me, I'm gone, okay?"

"In your own time," she says.

Cool customer. Doesn't sound fazed at all. I bet I do. I'm breathing all jerky, trying to stay calm, trying to stay Irish.

"I've got a license plate for you. Write it down."

I give her the details. Thank God I haven't forgotten them. I give her a description of the van, where it was parked, what the gobbos look like. I leave Paddy till last. Part of me wants to keep quiet about him. Part of me wants him to get away so I can have another go at him myself. I won't mess up a second time.

I know I won't.

But I tell her about him. Seems pointless not to.

"Have you got all that?" I say.

"Yes." First time she's spoken since I told her to shut up. "And you say this man's name's Paddy?"

"Yeah."

"Okay. So we're talking about six men but you only know two of the names—Paddy and Lenny. Is that right?"

"Yeah, and there's another thing about Paddy." I'm seeing his face again, seeing the wound I should have ripped across his throat, if only I hadn't spooked out. "There's . . . another thing about him."

"Yes?"

"His jaw might be broken."

"How did that happen?"

"He got hit by a cricket bat."

"Who by?"

I don't answer. I'm trying to think, trying to keep my accent from slipping, trying not to panic. I've told her too much cos my mind's fizzed.

"Who by?" she says.

Again I don't answer. I'm losing it again. I'm still drummed out of my head, picturing what I should have done to Paddy, what I can't believe I didn't do to Paddy.

Breathe, breathe, make yourself breathe. The woman speaks again.

"I've got everything written down but you haven't yet told me why this information's important."

Another breath. Long, slow. I make myself speak.

"The girl who got killed in the bungalow in Carnside."

"Yes?"

"You know about her?"

Stupid question. Course she knows. But she answers in the same quiet voice.

"I know about her."

"I've heard on the news you're looking for a boy called Slicky and a girl called Becky."

"That's correct. Is there any information you can give me?"

"I've seen Slicky. All the stuff I just told you—I got it from him."

"Where is he?"

"I haven't the faintest idea and I wouldn't tell you anyway. But listen—I know him a bit and he's not a murderer. He's just a wacky street kid. He told me he broke into the bungalow for a laugh and found the girl in there dead and this guy Paddy standing over her. And there was this other girl there too called Becky. Slicky and Becky got away and she told him later that Paddy killed Trixi. She didn't do it and Slicky didn't do it. Paddy did it. Are you listening to this?"

"Yes," says the woman.

I got to ring off. They've probably traced the call by now. Got to wig it out of here quick. But there's one more thing to say.

"Slicky told me another thing."

"And what's that?" she says.

"Paddy's now killed Becky as well. Hit her over the head or something. I couldn't get Slicky to tell me everything. He just said he was on the lane with Becky and her kid, and Paddy and those men caught up with them. The kid ran away and Paddy sorted Becky. Slicky ran off but he says he saw Becky get killed. Doesn't know what happened to her body. Could be just lying there or maybe dumped in one of the ditches. He wouldn't tell me any more. He just beat it. So you got to bring Paddy in and those other guys."

"All right. Now listen—"

"I got to go."

"Wait a minute, can you just tell me—"

"I got to go."

"Where's Slicky now?"

"That's all you're getting."

"Are you Slicky?"

I hang up. I'm shaking. I know I've messed this up bad. I wasn't thinking good, wasn't talking good. The accent kept slipping. There's no way that woman believed me.

But she'll follow this up. The porkers got tipped off last night about us being in the lane. They were there themselves. So they'll check this out. They might even bring in the gobbos and find Becky's body.

As for little Jaz . . .

That's something else I got to sort out. But to do that, I got to play stealth again. I got to leave Blade behind me, and Slicky too.

I got to become someone else.

32

NOW, THIS HOUSE IS A BIT DIFFERENT. It's not one of my nighttime snugs. I don't ever sleep here. Why? Cos there's a family who lives here and they don't go away much—at least, not enough to make it a safe place to snug out overnight.

Big crowd of 'em, noisy as hell. Mum, Dad and five boys. You got to feel for that woman. Nice enough family but sloppy as a custard pie. Leave stuff all over the place and they got no idea how to keep people out—not people like me anyway.

This is one of my daytime snugs. Haven't told you about them before. I got loads of 'em. More than I got nighttime snugs. Handy things, specially when I'm tired during the day and need a chill-pot for a few hours.

The great thing about this family is they're out most of the time. Monday to Friday, nine to five, there's nobody here. He's a bignob with the council, she's a dentist, the boys are at school.

Piece of cake getting in. They got a burglar alarm but they only had sensors put in the hall, front room and main bedroom. I suppose they think that's all they need. They've obviously got their valuables in those rooms.

But I'm not after their valuables. There's other stuff I want more and it's easy as spit to get at. Quick eye shine through the garage window to make sure they're all out.

No sweat. Both cars gone and all the bikes. Ring the front door just in case.

No answer.

Right, let's see which of the boys has left a window open this time. There's usually a couple at least. Come around the back.

What did I tell you?

One open there, another one there. Just a fraction and they probably think it doesn't show. You wouldn't believe how stupid some nebs are.

Check around. That's the other good thing about this place—no neighbors overlooking the front or the back of the house. But best to make sure nobody's sniffing about.

All clear.

Ladder from the shed, up against the wall. Another check, then up to the window. This room's shared by the twins. Dimpy kids, mad on soccer. Same age as me but a goofy-looking pair. Check around again, then whip through the window and pull it back like it was.

Easy.

Freeze and listen. Silence, just the ticking of the clock and the sound of traffic running past the end of the driveway. Nobody's in the house. Just me.

Me and my pain. Yeah, it's still there. I keep seeing Paddy's face. I had him, Bigeyes. He was finished. He was mine. Why isn't he dead?

He didn't get away. I let him go. I messed up.

Tick, tick, tick.

Bloody clock. I want to smash it up.

Tick, tick, tick.

Calm down. Talk to yourself. Talk aloud.

"Move your stump. Do what you got to do."

And there's more than one thing I got to do, so there's no time to waste.

"Move your stump."

Over to the door, check the landing. All quiet, apart from that effing clock. Down the landing, slow, easy, past the oldest boy's room, past the next two bedrooms, on to the top of the stairs. Got to be careful here. There's a sensor down in the hall.

It's never picked me up yet and the stairs are so high I could probably walk right past the gap, but I don't take any chances. Down and crawl. Keep below the level of the top step.

No problem.

Back on my feet and here's the bathroom. Careful again. Main bedroom's close. The door's usually shut but they've left it open this time. The sensor inside can't reach me here but I got to watch myself. I'm not thinking cute like I normally do. I'm too stressed up. I mustn't forget myself and walk past that sensor.

Just as well it's the bathroom we need first, or rather what's in the bathroom. Let's hope Mumsy hasn't used it all up.

I needn't have worried. She's got loads of the stuff left. Look at that shelf—totally crammed. She's even stocked up with more since I last came.

AUTUMN DREAMS

Permanent Conditioning Hair Color in 20 Minutes

Autumn Dreams? Who writes this stuff? It's hair dye, for God's sake. Still, as long as it works. Don't snigger, Bigeyes. I haven't done this before.

Nourishing multi-tonal color for rich, fade-resistant shine

I can't believe I'm reading this. Anyway, let's get on with it.

Scissors. There were two pairs in here last time, a small pair in the cabinet and another on the shelf.

No sign.

Look around—nothing.

Shit, I could do without this. I don't want to have to go looking. Hang on. . . .

Behind the shower gel—another pair. Dronky scissors, but they'll have to do. Right, coat off, sweater off, shirt off, lean over the basin—okay, now the scissors. . . .

Only they're not moving. Cos I'm not moving. I'm not doing anything. I'm just staring. I'm holding the scissors, like I held the knife in front of Paddy's face as he stared back at me, and here's another face doing just the same.

Staring back at me.

My own face in the mirror.

And you know what, Bigeyes? It looks even more scared than Paddy's did. And I'll tell you something else.

It's like looking at a face I've never seen before.

Yeah, I know—I've seen it. Hundreds of times, thousands of times. Every snug I go to's got a mirror. And every time I see a mirror, I check my face.

It's something I feel I got to do. Might sound dimpy but it's something I got to do. It's not cos I think my face is good.

It's cos I'm frightened it might be bad.

It never is. It's not good or bad. It's just clever. It's clever at not showing what I'm thinking or feeling. It's learned to do that without me trying. I'm fond of my face. It's a drawbridge. It keeps the world back, keeps me back.

Only not today. That's what's scary. Cos you know what's just happened?

The face has disappeared.

It's just me there instead. Me staring at me. And now the me in the glass is becoming more than just me. It's becoming other people as well. I can see Paddy, and Jaz, and the two Beckys, and Mary, and . . .

And all the other people.

I don't want to talk to 'em, Bigeyes. I don't want to see 'em.

"Go away, go away."

And there's my face again, like it used to be. Eyes, nose, mouth—everything just like it was. All the other stuff's gone. Thank God for that. I look down at the scissors, snip 'em in the air.

They'll do. Autumn Dreams'll do. And so will I.

I'll do.

33

WHAT DO YOU RECKON, BIGEYES? Too much off the back? I'm a bit worried I've made it too short. But you got to admit the color's good.

Not quite sure where Autumn Dreams come in. It's red-brown as far as I'm concerned, same as Mumsy's hair. Still, who cares what it's called? It's different and that's all I'm bothered about.

Okay, next step.

Back to the twins' bedroom. The great thing about this family is they never use half the stuff they got—and they got loads, as you can see. And cos it's all so untidy, they'll never miss the things I'm going to take. Even if they do, they'll probably just think they've lost 'em.

Right, we need an empty plastic bag. There's always gobs of 'em in this house. They buy stuff from the supermarket or wherever and just leave the bags all over the place. I saw one under the bed by the window when I climbed in.

There it is. Perfect. Nice and big too. Hang on—there's something inside it.

Girlie mag.

Typical. We'll have to use another bag. This is definitely one the boys won't have forgotten and they'll know straight-away someone's taken it. They'll probably think Mumsy's been poking about and that'll freak 'em out but best not to leave any clues, even the wrong ones.

Check around the room.

Can't see any other bags I can use. We'll try the oldest boy's room. He's always buying games and stuff for his computer. He should have something we can use.

Bingo, loads of bags. We'll take that green one. Back to the bathroom, shove the loose hair into the bag, wash the tiny bits down the plughole, dry around the basin, put everything back as it was.

Now the clothes Mary gave me.

Feels kind of weird getting rid of 'em. Don't know why. But I keep thinking of the old girl, keep remembering how I let her down. But I got to trade the clothes, like I had to trade my hair.

They won't all go in the bag. The coat and the sweater go in, and the shirt, just. No room for the rest.

Back to the big lad's room, grab another bag. I'm tempted to cream one of his jackets while I'm here but it's probably too big, and anyway, he's more tidy than the others. He'll notice it's gone.

The twins won't miss anything apart from the girlie mag. All that stuff and you know what, Bigeyes? Most of it's exactly like it was the last time I came, and the time before that.

Not cos they use it and put it back where it was, but cos they don't use it. They don't even think about it.

Don't ask me how I know.

Okay, back to the twins' room. Off with the trousers, socks, shoes. Stuff 'em in the second bag. Right, we got to go for something different from Mary's clothes, something dead different.

And it's got to be things the twins haven't touched for yonks and won't miss.

Open the wardrobe. Check that out, Bigeyes. See what I mean? What's the point having all those clothes if you don't wear 'em? And I'm telling you, they don't. When I see those kids around, they're either in school uniforms or tracksuits.

That's it. They don't wear anything else. And I haven't even shown you the stuff they got inside the wall cupboard and the chest of drawers. But I probably won't need to. There's enough here in front of me.

Right, let's get on with it. Shirt, trousers, belt, socks, shoes, sweater.

How easy was that? Try 'em on.

Good fit too. Better than the clothes Mary gave me. Even the shoes don't pinch like I thought they would. Just need a couple more things.

Jacket with a hood.

Nothing too flash. Got to be boring so it doesn't draw attention. Not much in here. Try the wall cupboard. Yeah, this'll do. Gray anorak. Yucky but it fits neat. I'll have it. Now the last thing.

Glasses.

Both boys wear 'em and I don't, so I won't be able to use 'em much without spooking my eyes. But they might come in handy. The boys have got loads of spare pairs in their desk drawers.

Don't ask me why. They must keep their old glasses every time they go to the optician for some new ones. See? Three pairs in this drawer and two in that one.

I'll try 'em all.

This pair'll do. Bit blurry but I can always tip 'em down my nose and peer over the top. I'll take 'em anyway. Shove 'em in the jacket pocket next to the knife.

Shit!

I've gone all cold, Bigeyes. I'm standing here and I'm frozen up like I'm made of ice. Cos you know what?

I'm touching the knife but I don't remember shifting it.

I don't remember taking it out of my old pocket and putting it in this one. Sounds stupid. I know it does. Stupid to worry, I mean. You don't remember everything you do. You just do stuff and don't notice. It's no big deal.

And this should be no big deal.

Only it feels like one. I don't know why.

I pull out the knife, feel it, stare at it. I don't flick it open. I just hold it, look at it. And suddenly it's like I want to yank open the window and throw the effing thing out into the garden, throw it as far away as I can.

Only it won't be far enough. You know why? Cos no matter where I throw it, it'll find me again. It always does. Don't ask me how I know.

I squeeze the knife, put it back in my pocket. And suddenly I'm glad I didn't jack it. Cos I still got a use for it. If I can just get my brain stitched, I can do what I should have done last night.

I can sort Paddy.

Cos I got to. It's right, not just for Becky but for me. I got to prove myself again. I can't be weak next time. I got to prove myself. If I can just find the guts.

Guts.

Tiny little word for such a big thing. Bit like *fear.* Another tiny word, another big thing. And you know what, Bigeyes? It's making me wonder.

Making me wonder if I dare do the thing I really want to do, the thing I always want to do when I snug out here, specially when I'm scared. Trouble is, I'm going to need guts for that too.

Cos to do what I want to do, what I really ache to do, I got to go past the main bedroom, past the open door, past the sensor.

Yeah, I know. It's a spitty idea. It's so risky I'd be bung-crazy to try it. I already got what I came for today. It's time to split, not moon about.

But already I'm walking down the landing. I can't stop myself, Bigeyes. I'm past the oldest boy's room, past the next two, past the bathroom, and here's the open door of the main bedroom, and beyond it, at the end of the landing . . .

The study.

Door open too. I can see right in from here. I can see the books on the shelves. They look like jewels. I haven't read 'em all. But I've looked inside each one. I know 'em in my own way, like I know all the books in all the snugs I go to.

In my own way.

I'm looking at treasure, Bigeyes. It's glistening back at me. I can see *Sherlock Holmes* and *David Copperfield* and *Jane Eyre,* and that book on the Andes with the photograph of the condors, and *Tao Te Ching,* and *The Diary of Samuel Pepys,* and *Swallows and Amazons.*

Swallows and Amazons.

I love that book. It's a stinger. I can see the cover, the title at the top of the spine, the picture underneath, the author's name in capital letters: ARTHUR RANSOME.

Must have been well brained-up, that gobbo. His book's so good I only have to see the cover and I'm on the lake with John and Susan and Nancy and all the other characters. But it's not enough, not right now. I don't just want to see the cover.

I want to read the book. I want to read it so bad it stuns me.

I hate water. I'm scared of it cos it's big and moving and I can't control it. I don't even want to learn to swim. I just want to stay away from it. But when I read *Swallows and Amazons,* it's like I'm sailing and swimming and everything's plum.

And I want to read it now. I want to forget what's happening for a while. I want to dive into the story, and sail and swim and not be scared. It's worth the risk. The sensor won't get me if I'm quick.

I wait, brace myself, check the gap—jump.

The alarm screams out at once.

34

Stupid tick! Stupid bloody tick! What the hell was I thinking?

Back to the twins' room, grab the two bags, push open the window. No sign of anybody below but there's bound to be someone coming to check the house. Out the window, close it like it was, down the ladder, look around.

Still nobody. Then a voice.

"Hello?"

Some guy calling from the front of the house. Sounds old and nervous. I only just heard him with the alarm going. He hasn't appeared yet, so I might still get away if I'm quick.

Whip the ladder back to the shed, slip behind it out of sight, check around the side.

Ancient gobbo standing by the gate. Looks creaky on his feet and he's clearly unsure whether to come around the back of the house. Hasn't seen me yet but he will if I move.

Got to wait. Got to stay put.

Only I can't stay put for long. I got to split. If other nebs turn up, I'm in the grime.

He's coming forward, dead slow, watching all about him. Looks scared, like he's not sure he should be doing this. I'm whispering to him.

"Go back, Creaky. Nothing for you around here."

But he's coming on. I stay put, keep watching.

He's stopped at the edge of the house, peering this way

and that. Definitely nearsighted but he's looking around, checking the garden, checking the house.

"Go back, Creaky."

The alarm's still screeching away. Sounds demented. I feel like a claphead. Can't believe I was so stupid. I should never have taken such a risk. I should have left the books alone and blasted out sweet and good while I had the chance.

And here's more trouble—another man's voice from the front of the house.

"Jim? You there?"

Just what I bloody need. Creaky's turned.

"I'm in the back garden!"

The other gobbo appears. About thirty, chunky build. Looks a bit handy. Joins Creaky and they both look over the back of the house. And now a third voice.

"Jim?"

A woman this time. She's at the gate before they can answer. About the same age as Chunky. She's holding a mobile phone.

"We're here!" calls Creaky.

She comes around and joins them in the back garden.

"Any trouble?" she says.

"Can't see anything," says Chunky.

"Then move off," I whisper. "Move bloody off."

They don't move off. They spread out, Creaky toward the far end of the garden, the woman over to the French windows, Chunky toward the shed.

This is getting bad, Bigeyes. I'm still out of sight but if he keeps coming on, I'm stuffed. Then the woman calls out.

"There!"

But she's not pointing at me. She's pointing up at the twins' bedroom. Chunky stops and turns.

"The window," she says. "It's slightly open."

Both gobbos stare up at it.

"Might have been like that before," says Creaky. "You know what the boys are like."

"There are some marks in the grass," says the woman. She bends over them. "Like someone's dug the end of a ladder in it."

Creaky steps over and looks down.

"We don't know for certain it's ladder marks."

"Easy to check," says Chunky. "They keep it in the shed."

And he turns back toward me.

"I'm going to ring Mr. Braden," says the woman. "I've got his work number."

"And then the police," says Creaky.

"I'll check out the ladder," says Chunky, and he comes on again.

I tense. If I stay where I am, he'll see me the moment he reaches the door. If I move to the side to avoid him, I'll put myself in sight of the other two.

But now there are more shouts from the front of the house.

Men's voices.

"Everything all right back there?"

"Need any help?"

No sign of anybody at the gate, but Chunky's stopped, inches from the door. He's turned to look back, and so have the others. Now's my chance, while they're facing the other way.

I fling the bags over the fence into the next garden, then scramble up after them. I try to make it a jump, a vault, but the fence is too high and I have to rough it over. They hear me and turn.

All of 'em, including the two new gobbos who've just poked in from the driveway.

"Over there!" shouts one.

I drop into the other garden, grab the bags and jet it across the lawn. Great big thing with apple trees down the sides and a pond in the middle. The house is a long way down and just as well. I'm hoping nobody there's heard the shouting, even if they've snagged the sound of the alarm.

No sign of anyone at the windows yet but I'm checking 'em good as I belt on.

I'm not looking back at all. I've jerked the hood over my head and I'm wigging it as fast as I can go. Not fast enough though.

"There he is!" comes a shout behind me.

And now there's a face at one of the upstairs windows.

An old dunny peering out at me. Looks frightened. She's holding a phone and dialing a number. A young man appears next to her, then another, then a boy.

They disappear from view as I tear down the side of the house. I hear shouts from inside.

"I'll cut him off at the front!"

One of the guys but I don't stop to think. I reach the front of the house. Nobody there yet but I can hear footsteps pounding on the staircase. There's a mountain bike propped outside the front door. Got to be the boy's.

"Thanks, mate."

I hook the bags onto the handlebars, shove the bike out

of the gate. The front door bursts open and the two guys thunder out.

"Hoy!" bellows one.

But I'm already pedaling like death.

More shouts behind me, some from the gobbos in the doorway, some from Chunky. He's run all the way around to where the driveway meets the street. Yelling either side of me too, doors and windows opening right and left.

Sound of a car starting behind me.

Got to get off the street.

Another car starting.

I look about me. I know this place. There's an alley just ahead that runs down the side of the children's playground. I put on speed. Revving behind me, the roar of engines. They'll be here in seconds but here's the playground, here's the alley.

Young woman blocking the way, bending over a little girl. Cute kid, Jaz's age. Mum's fixing her coat for her. I hear the engines close behind.

"Get out of the way!" I scream.

Mum looks up, stares in horror.

The engines grow louder.

"Get out of the way!"

She bundles the kid to the side. I shoot off the road and into the alley. Behind me I hear brakes screech, doors slam, then shouts from the men, screams from the woman, burning like hate inside my head.

I pedal on and don't look back.

35

TWO MINUTES LATER I'm through the alley and racing down Westbury Drive. Nobody after me but I can't stick around here. Anyone who knows where the alley leads can work out where I am. I got to get off the road quick.

Not yet though. Nowhere to dive just here. I got to get to Merton Crescent, take the footpath toward the allotments and dump the gear. After that I know what I got to do.

No compromise there.

Nothing's changed, Bigeyes. I might be drummed out of my head and making mistakes but I'm still guffed over Bex and Jaz. I'm still breathing blood over Paddy.

Here's Merton Crescent.

So far, so good. No sign of pursuit, no funny looks from people in the street. Down to the end, through the gap to the footpath, off the bike.

Got to be careful now. Got to fade into the air, leave no pictures behind. The anorak's a problem. I still got the hood up, so no one's seen much of my face or hair, but Chunky or Creaky are bound to report the jacket.

So I got to sort that.

Bike against the wall, check around. All quiet on the footpath. Nip back to the gap, peer around Merton Crescent. Sleepy little road but I don't trust the windows. Too watchful.

Back to the bike, wheel it farther down the footpath, stop

again. Check both ways. Nobody in sight. Check over the walls. Back gardens either side, nobody in 'em.

House on the left looks empty. Windows closed, no lights, no noise. Feels pretty safe. Other one's got the back door open. Grab the carrier bags, lean the bike against the wall, check around again.

Looks good.

Over the wall into the first garden, down the side of the house, open the garbage can. Couldn't be better—half full, mostly garbage bags. Take off the anorak, pull out the glasses, pull out the knife.

And there's that feeling again.

Shit, Bigeyes, am I going to get this every time I touch a knife? I never used to. I just did what I did and it was a whack. Now I'm shivering and seeing Paddy gibbering at me in the darkness.

I don't want to see that scumbo's face. And if I got to see it, I don't want to see it like it was last night. I want to see it like it's going to be when I've finished with him.

A dead face, a ripped-up face. Cos you better believe it, Bigeyes, that's how it's going to be. If I can just zap it.

Slip the knife into my trouser pocket, pull out some of the garbage bags, check around again. No sounds from inside the house, no sign of anyone watching. Drop the jacket and carrier bags into the can, shove 'em right down, dump the garbage bags on top.

Perfect. Looks just like it did.

Close the lid, put on the glasses, tip 'em down so I can see over the top. Back to the footpath, wheel the bike toward the allotments.

I know what you're thinking, Bigeyes. You're thinking why

keep the bike when they saw that too? Well, you can go on thinking. I don't have to explain everything to you.

All right, stop glumming. I'll tell you.

I need the bike a bit longer, okay? Risky, I know, but I got some distance to go and time's ticking. We'll have to walk past the allotments but once they're behind us, I can ride. And if I keep to the quiet roads, I should be all right.

Allotments opening up already, see? Nice and empty, apart from that old gobbo at the far end and he's just a muffin. Even so, I got to keep a good watch. Walk on, sniping around. No sign of any trouble but I'm feeling edgy.

Bike's making a noise, kind of a tickety-tick. Twig caught in the spokes. Bend down, pull it out, straighten up, see two figures ahead.

Gobbos.

Middle-aged and probably muffins but I'm watching 'em cute. They're coming on. I push the bike forward, not too fast, not too slow. They're looking me over. I know what's coming. One of 'em's going to ask me why I'm not in school.

But I'm wrong.

They're past and gone without a word.

On down the footpath and through to Cutnall Drive. Back on the bike and away, out to the main road, over that and off down the lanes toward the eastern suburbs.

It's getting colder and I'm starting to miss that jacket. Sky's darker too. More rain coming. I put on speed. Need to get there before it comes down.

But it's already spitting.

Into the Cliffsea estate, past the shops, down Langdon

Drive, onto the track by the soccer field. Down to the end, stop by the bushes, check around.

No sign of anyone. Check again, check good. All clear.

Heave the bike into the bushes.

I kick it well under the foliage and step back. Good and buried. You can't see it at all from the track. You'd have to walk right up to the bushes and even then you might miss it.

Got to move. Rain's getting heavier. Just as well we haven't got far to go. Over the stile and left down the lane toward Marsh View.

Don't ask me why they call it that. There's nothing in the way of marsh around here and not much of a view either. But it's not a bad name for a smelly block of flats on the backside of an estate.

Cos that's what it is. See it? That dronky building is Marsh View.

And I'll tell you something else, Bigeyes.

It's where I was bringing us last night. The place I wouldn't tell Bex about. You were probably wondering why, like she was.

Well, I had a plan. Or kind of a plan.

I could still use it for myself if I wanted to. To get away, I mean. Only we both know I won't. That plan's stuffed now, so I'll use it for something else.

Okay, walk on. Got to be super-cute now. Got to walk small, walk dark, walk invisible. Best no one sees us come and go. And if they do, best they don't remember us. So watch out. It's a funny little estate. Mostly sleepers but there's nosy nebs here too.

Close now. Keep walking, head down, low and slow, easy pace. Snipe left and right. Just as well it's raining. Nobody out now apart from those two women on the other sidewalk, and they're hurrying away.

Can't use these glasses anymore. They're doing my head in, specially now that they're wet. Chuck 'em in the trash, walk on, nice and slow, nice and casual. Here we are.

Marsh End.

What did I tell you, Bigeyes? Dronky or what? You'd have to be brain-dead to live in a place like this. Lucky for us, there's one guy who is. But we're not here to see his flat.

We're here to nick his car.

36

NEVER MIND how I'm going to do it. Just shut up and keep watch.

Okay, around the back of the building, down the row of garages. We want the one at the end. Should be unlocked, unless he's got himself organized and fixed the door, which isn't likely. He's one disorganized gobbo.

Keep low. We can't relax just cos it's raining and there's no one out. There's windows looking down on these garages. See 'em? Nebs live in there, nebs with eyes and yakky mouths.

I'm just hoping no one's looking out right now. Can't see anyone but we won't hang about. Right, here's the end garage. Check the door. What did I tell you?

Unlocked.

Know why? Cos two years ago I squirted a bit of superglue in the fitting. Not so you'd notice it—or he wouldn't anyway—but enough to bodge the mechanism. Door closes okay but it won't lock. He still hasn't got around to fixing it.

Not that I come here much. I only use the garage if my usual snugs are taken and I'm desperate for a doss. I break in here and sleep in the car. It's warmer and comfier than slapping it on the street with the other duffs. Easier too.

Cos he never locks his car either.

Pull up the garage door, nip inside, pull it down again. Good to be out of the rain, good to be hidden again. Don't touch the light switch, Bigeyes. We mustn't be seen. And anyway, I like the darkness. I need it right now. And I can see good enough.

Check out the car.

Eyesore, isn't it? Not quite a banger but give it a few months. Main thing is, it'll do the job. It's old, it's got no alarm, and it still looks just about legal so hopefully the porkers'll leave us alone.

The gobbo who owns it hardly uses it. How do I know? Cos I check the milo every time I come. And you know what?

It's only moved ten in the last twelve months. That's right—ten miles. I've been keeping the score. The gas gauge has been three-quarters full for yonks.

Two years ago he used to drive it a bit more. Not far—just little trips—but enough to stack up the milo. This last year's been different. He's hardly touched the thing. Took me a while to find out why.

He's got a gammy leg.

He's an old gobbo, lives alone on the ground floor, doesn't get out much cos he can't. Shouldn't really have a car. There's no way he's safe on the road. He probably knows that but he's keeping it anyway, like lots of old gobbos hang on to stuff.

And that suits me.

Cos if he can't use the car, I can.

Haven't driven it before. I've just used it for the comfy seats and extra warmth when I've had to slap it for the night. But now it's time to let her loose. Okay, open the door. Shouldn't be a problem. Like I say, he never locks it.

Shit, I don't believe it. Won't open. Try the other door.

Locked too.

What's going on? He must have come out here for something—not to drive, that's for sure—and then locked the door after him.

Never mind, we can sort it. He's got everything we need in this little den. If we can just find it in the dark. Check around the far corner. That's where he keeps his tools and stuff. Bit of a tip but it's all there.

Piece of wire, that's what we want.

This bit's too long. Check around. He had some cutters here last time. There they are. Right, trim the wire, bend it into shape.

Perfect.

Driver's door, pull back the rubber around the window, squeeze the wire down the gap. Come on, you dimp, go in. Got it. Poke it down, feel for the catch.

This is stupid, Bigeyes. I'm losing my touch. I should be in the car by now. But I suppose I haven't done much of this for a while. When I was playing dead and keeping low, I just wanted to stay under the radar.

So I'm out of practice.

Click!

Gotcha. Open the door. Now, back to the tools. We want a screwdriver. Got to be the right type. This'll do. Jump in the car. Stinky bloody thing, isn't it? What's this under the driver's seat?

A woolly hat.

That wasn't here last time. And the flashlight is gone. He used to keep it under the dashboard. Maybe that's what he came out to the car for. He leaned down, grabbed the flashlight, dropped his hat at the same time, then locked the doors and went.

Whatever.

I can use the hat anyway. Yeah, I know. Dronky but I need to keep changing the way I look. And that gives me another idea.

He used to keep an old overcoat in the garage.

There it is, hanging on a nail by the door.

Jump out, put it on. Bit cobwebby but it's warm and most of all it's old-fashioned. Got a hood too. Even better. Can't do any harm. Okay, Bigeyes, this is it. We got to start her up. But we'll keep the door closed till the last minute. Right, screwdriver . . .

Dig it under the plastic surround on the steering column. Easy peasy. It's loose anyway. I love these old motors. Pull it off. Now, screwdriver again. We got to pry off the ignition switch.

Doesn't want to come. Shift, you bastard! Come off!

There it goes—one sweet little ignition switch.

Now for the hard work. We got to yank the wheel till we break the steering lock. I like this bit normally. Makes me feel good. Don't know why.

But I'm different about this one.

Maybe it's the gobbo. I've never spoken to him. He doesn't even know I exist. But it's like most of the nebs I watch. I feel like I know 'em. Some of 'em I don't care about. I just use their snugs, eat their food, read their books.

But this old guy—seems kind of nice. Bit spittled in the head but no mess to anybody. I feel a bit bad nicking his motor. Still, he doesn't need it anymore.

And I do. Can't be sentimental about it.

Yank, yank, yank. This is going to be a scrap, Bigeyes. It doesn't want to go. Yank, yank, yank. It's not going to go, it's not going to go.

CRACK!

You beauty!

Out of the car, push open the garage door. Rain's heavier than it was. Suits me fine. Check around the site. Nobody outside, nobody watching, as far as I can see. But even if they are, we're going.

Back to the car, jump in, force the screwdriver into the ignition switch. Perfect fit. Like they were made for each other. Hold your breath, Bigeyes. This is the moment. It should work. It usually works. Choke out, twist the screwdriver and . . .

The engine roars into life.

Rev up, give her a minute, ease back the choke. Reverse gear—think it's push down and right. Got it. Hand brake off, clutch up. She's a juddery girl, this one, a skitty old dingo. But she's moving, slow, out of the garage.

Rain's spattered the back window already. Can't be bothered to look for the rear wiper. There's plenty of room behind me. But it's spuming down now.

We're outside. Check around. Nobody in sight.

Jump out, close the garage door, back in the car. Fiddle around for the wiper control. Found it. We're clear to go. And still nobody in sight.

Come on, Bigeyes. We got things to do.

37

DRIVES ALL RIGHT, this girl. Bit of a scraggy clutch but okay once you get to know it. Wish I could open her up, do some damage. I want to rag her till she screams. Might make me feel better.

But it's too risky. And this isn't a joyride. It's business. It's keep to the speed limit, drive steady, no mess. We don't want eyeballs on us. That's where the rain's helping. Hard to see out, hard to see in, and nobody much interested in us anyway.

Out of the estate and down Strickland Lane. I know what you're thinking. You're thinking why head for the bypass and not into the city? Well, tough. Think till your brain pops. You'll find out soon enough. I got other stuff to sort out.

If I can just get the radio working.

Haven't used it before. Never wanted to take the risk of being heard in the garage. Just hope it works. Clock says it's close on one, so we should get something on one of the local channels.

"The news at one o'clock."

Bingo.

"Police are still looking for a boy of about fourteen, known by the nickname Slicky, and a sixteen-year-old girl named Rebecca Jakes in connection with the murder of teenager Trixi Kenton."

They haven't found Bex. Shit, Bigeyes, she's still lying in a ditch.

"There have been fresh developments during the day. Following an incident in the early hours of the morning, police are now investigating a deserted van, though they are not confirming whether or not this has any connection with the missing pair. In a separate incident later this morning, a boy in a gray anorak was seen running from the back garden of a house in the Hamforth area of the city. Police are very anxious to trace this boy, though they are not saying whether there is any link between him and the boy they are hunting in connection with the murder."

No mention of Jaz at all.

I'll tell you what it means, Bigeyes. It means Paddy and the other gobbos are still free. Well, maybe it's what I wanted, sort of. Not the grunt and those other dregs. I could have done with them bobbed up.

But Paddy—I want him for myself. I want a second chance. And this time I'll get it right.

Left toward the bypass, right down Southlands Avenue. Radio's still on. They're talking about other stuff. I'm trying to think, trying to stay calm.

It's hard. Got me worked up again hearing all this. I keep wondering about Bex. I hate to think of her body getting wet.

And Jaz.

I keep thinking about her too.

Switch off the radio. Don't want to hear any more. Got to focus, got to stop spinning my head. Got to think what I'm doing or I'm bogged out. End of Southlands Avenue and here's another plug in my heart.

The junction with Britannia Road.

Right takes me out of the city. Five miles and I'm on the motorway and gone. Plenty of gas. I could scrape it a long way before I dump the car. Only it's no good.

We've been through this, Bigeyes. We both know I'm not going.

Turn left. Do what you got to do. Off down the road, around the roundabout, and now it gets interesting. Cos this is where I'm going to blitz your mind, Bigeyes. You were starting to think you knew me a bit, right?

Don't shake your head. You were. Well, get ready to be amazed.

Down the road, past the school, past the shops, left at the end. See that lane? Leads off into the country. Runs for a couple of miles through fields and stuff and ends up at a little stream.

Remote spot.

And that's where we're going.

Yeah, I know. I got this fear of water. Okay, this terror. I admit it. I don't mind having a shower or a bath in some snug cos I'm in control when I do that. I turn on the tap and I turn it off again. A river's a different thing if it's a big one like down by the docks. So's a lake. I keep away from stuff like that. And I don't even want to think about the sea.

But this stream's no bum gripe, first cos it's not that deep and second cos we're not going on the water or in it. Well, not really, not so it's a problem. Come on. I'll show you.

Down the lane, slow, steady. Nothing too jumpy. Not that there's much risk. Nobody comes this way much. That's why I chose it. And the rain's going to keep off any hard-crust fishermen.

I hope.

Got caught out once. Guy in long wellies, wouldn't shift. Had to wait for hours till he split. That's why I normally come here at night.

I need the place to myself. Too right I do.

Drive on, still slow. Dingo car's juddering again. Doesn't like the low gears. Like I say, I usually come here at night. And I don't drive. I nick a bike and ride out here. Only not all the way.

See that stile ahead? On the left, where the stone wall's a bit loose? Just past that there's a willow, then some bushes on the other side of the wall. You'll catch 'em in a moment.

There you go. Got 'em?

I heave the bike over the wall out of sight among the bushes, and walk the rest of the way. That's why we're stopping the car. Engine off, climb out. Rain's eased off. Nice timing.

Right, Bigeyes, we walk the rest of the way. No glumming. We walk.

No connection with the car. No connection with anything. Just a boy walking down a lane and hopefully no one to see him.

Let's go.

Down the lane, slow as before, steady and slow. Dark, swirly sky, rain clouds but dry for the moment. Let's hope it stays like that a bit longer. We don't need much time. But a dry patch would be cute.

Last part of the lane. Twisting ahead, see? Another few yards and you'll hear the stream. Nice kind of sound, specially at night when there's a moon out, and maybe stars, and it's all quiet. I don't come here a lot but when I do, I like to hear the sound of the stream.

Makes the water feel less scary. Not much though. Follow the bend around to the right. Listen. . . .

Got it? Okay, bit farther—now listen. . . .

That's it. Soft, trickly sound. It's usually a bit louder. Maybe it's the breeze keeping it low. Come on, and keep your eyes moving. We should be alone but you got to watch. And remember what I said.

I'm going to blitz your mind.

You're going to be amazed.

There's the stream. Sweet little thing, isn't it, considering it's effing water. Walk to the end of the lane, turn right along the bank. Keep sniping around.

Looks all clear, like it usually is. I'd still rather have come here at night but we haven't got that luxury today. It's got to be now.

Okay, nearly there. See that narrow bridge ahead? Tiny little thing half hidden by gorse? It's only for walkers. It links that path coming from the right with the one on the other bank.

That's where the fisherman was standing that day.

And it's where we're heading now.

But slow like before, watching like before. We got to be more careful than ever now. Cos there's lots to lose if we get this wrong.

Up to the little bridge, stop, check around. Now—climb down the bank, dip under. Bank falls away into the stream. Only what else do you see?

Three things.

First, the water's shallow—knee-height max. Second, the underside of the bridge is made of brick. Third, it's all nice and solid.

Only you'd be wrong.

Shoes off, socks off, roll up the trousers. Don't like this bit, Bigeyes. I know it's only shallow. I know I said it's not a bum gripe. But I still don't like it. What if I slipped over and hit my head on something? You can drown in a bath, remember. It's happened. I have to keep telling myself it's safe.

Brace up . . . into the water. Yi! It's got a chill like a frozen kiss.

"Come on, front up. Get used to it. Can't hurt me."

That's it. Keep saying it. Can't hurt me, can't hurt me. It's too shallow. I just wish it would stop ripping against my legs.

Focus. Do what you got to do.

Right, Bigeyes, look ahead. Check out the underside of the bridge. See the brickwork? Follow it down to about three feet above the water. Now check out the bricks again. What do you see?

Nothing. I can tell. You see beautiful bricks. An expert piece of building.

Now watch.

This one here . . . waggle it. Tiny bit loose. See? Bit more, now ease it out, slow, slow. Not too violent or we'll chew up the edge and make it clear the brick comes out. Got to be clever about this. Took me ages to make it look right.

There we go—out it comes. What do you see inside? A little empty space. That's cos I've taken out some of the other bricks. You've heard of a hole in the wall, right? Well, this is mine. And it's better than any bank.

Reach in, feel about, pull out the plastic bag.

Surprised? I knew you would be.

Check inside it. What do you find? Another plastic bag. And inside that . . . another one. And inside that . . .

Over ten grand.

There's work gone into getting that, Bigeyes. Lots of work over lots of time. And it's not from lifting wallets. I'm hot crack when it comes to that but there's other ways of making money.

And I got plenty. This isn't my only secret cupboard. There's more. I'm not telling you where. But I will tell you something. There's not just money in 'em.

Go on, reach in again, right to the bottom.

Another plastic bag.

Pull it out. Same again, bags inside bags. And what do you find at the end? Go on, tell me you're not blitzed.

Diamonds.

38

And they're not just any diamonds. Look at 'em. When did you see jewels like that? You probably never been this close to so much beauty. Or so much wealth.

Yeah, wealth. We're talking wealth, Bigeyes. The kind of wealth some people kill for. And remember what I said—this isn't my only cupboard.

Okay, I've shown you. And now we put it back. That's right, we put it back. Can't take it with us. Too risky. You can't carry this stuff around with you. It stays hidden for another time. I came here for the ten grand.

Push the diamonds back in the cupboard, check the money again. Didn't want to have to break into this. I've been living good enough off what I lift. I was saving this for emergencies.

Well, this is an emergency. I got to do what I got to do, and then wig it out of the city. Got to hit someplace I don't know that well and where I got to stay low. And I may have someone with me. I won't be able to nip out and cream wallets anytime I feel like it.

I'm shivering in the water now. I want to climb out but I got to stay hidden under the bridge while I finish this off. Quick count of the money.

Ten thousand, four hundred and sixty pounds.

How much to take, that's the question.

The lot. Take the lot. There's plenty more elsewhere. It's just that . . . I'm a bit cautious carrying so much, especially where I'm going. But then, maybe I just got to risk it. There might not be a chance to clock one of the other cupboards. I may have to blast out too quick.

And I'll need all the money I can find.

Take the lot.

Split up the money, push different bits into different pockets. My hand brushes the knife, closes around it. I feel another shiver. It's not like the shiver from the water. It's a different shiver. I let go of the knife, pull my hand out.

"Come on. Get on with it."

I stuff the empty bags back in the cupboard, wedge the brick in place again, check all's cute. Looks like it always did, nice and neat. And now—at last—out of this stinking water.

Up the bank, dripping, cold. Check around. Nobody in sight. All quiet. Just the breeze ruffling the grass and the trees along the top. Stop on the path, roll my trousers back down, pull on my socks and shoes.

Check again.

Still quiet.

Set off back down the lane. And now I'm getting nervous, Bigeyes. I don't want to choke out but I'm getting stressed. It's not just cos I don't like carrying all this money.

It's cos of the knife.

Just touching it again's brought everything back. It's not going to stop me from going through with things. Don't stick that idea in your pot. When it comes to it, you'll see what I am. I messed up before. It won't happen again.

Only this is it.

This is where it happens.

Reach the car, check all's clear, jump in, start up. No room to turn here or close to the stream. Hit reverse, ease the clutch. Bit of a judder but the old dame starts to move. I'm getting a cricky neck peering back but there's nothing else for it till we find a place to turn.

This gate'll do.

Back off the lane, change gear, forward, around, off. We're heading for the city.

And my thoughts are flying.

I should be thinking of my plan, thinking of what's going on around me, but I'm not. I'm thinking of the past. Those diamonds set me off. Never mind where they came from. It's none of your business.

But they set me off.

Set me thinking of Becky. Not the Becky lying in a ditch but the other Becky. My old sweet Becky. She shouldn't have died. She should be alive. Why does everybody I care for have to die?

She'd have been my age if she'd lived.

Think of that. Fourteen. Still a kid really, like me. Only she never made it past eleven. And the other Becky didn't do much better. Sixteen, like Trixi was. Still a kid too, sort of. And then Mary.

No kid, that's for sure.

But just as dead.

They all die, Bigeyes. One by one they slip away. What's going to happen to me? Am I going to slip away too? Maybe I'll be dead as well by the end of the day, money gone, dreams gone.

But I never had much in the way of dreams anyway.

I should have. Everybody should have dreams. That's why I like stories. They're all about dreams. Dreams of being someone else, somewhere else. In stories you can be anything you want. Just for a while, a few minutes or hours. You can escape.

But not now.

This isn't a story. And it's certainly not a dream.

It's starting to rain again. I'm glad. It'll help. Cos I got to stop blabbing now, got to start watching. We're in the outskirts but I want to keep to the quiet streets. I know how to get where I want to go.

But we won't be alone. Remember that. There's other people'll be there too.

Paddy's not stupid. He'll know it's one of two things. Either I blasted out the city or I stayed. And if I stayed, then there's only one thing I'd stay for. And he'll know what that is.

What he won't know is that my hair's different, my clothes are different, I'm in a car. And that I'm still hunting him.

He won't know that.

Till it's too late.

More rain. I like it. I trust it. It's like the darkness. You can trust the darkness. You can stay hidden.

Drive on, sniping left and right. Traffic building up as we head in. Check the clock. Quarter past three. Were we that long sorting the money?

Doesn't matter. It's now that matters and now's dangerous enough. What's worrying me is the porkers. Seen three police cars in the last two minutes. No fuss with any of 'em but I got to be careful, got to drive right.

Another two police cars. Jesus, Bigeyes, they're out in

force. I suppose I should have guessed. Trixi dead, gobbos on the loose, me on the loose. Maybe they've found Bex's body, maybe even Mary's. No wonder they're buzzing around.

Drive on, street after street. Two porkers standing outside the Royal Oak. They turn and watch as I pass. Check the mirror—they're staring after me. I got a bad feeling, Bigeyes. I got a really bad feeling.

Left onto Sampson Street, down to the end, right at the crossroads. On, on. We're going too fast. I don't mean the speed. That's legal, that's perfect. I mean the time. It's moving too quick.

Cos I don't want to arrive. Not yet. I don't want to be there. But the minutes are falling faster than the rain. On, on, street after street. I can feel my anger building up again. It's mixing with the fear and I don't like it. I know this mix too well. It's like a cocktail.

Only you wouldn't want to drink it.

Anger and fear, anger and fear. I've felt those two all my life. I can handle one at a time. Put 'em together and I'm trouble.

I'm dangerous.

Already I'm feeling for the knife. It's in my pocket pressed against some of the money. I pull it out, one hand on the steering wheel.

"Put it back. Not now."

But talking makes no difference. I don't put it back. I flick it open. I'm steering with my left hand, feeling the blade with my right. And I'm murmuring to myself.

"Paddy, Paddy, Paddy. . . ."

I close the blade, slip the knife back in my pocket. Cos now I've seen something else—the entrance to Elmleigh Drive.

Where the old dunny lives. Remember her, Bigeyes? Tammy's gran. If they're keeping Jaz anywhere, it'll be here. Only we got to be spiky now. Got to miss nothing. Cos we're not just watching the house. We're watching for the nebs who are watching for us.

Trust me, they're here. Can't see 'em but they're here. Don't ask me how I know.

Drive down, slow, normal, park at the end behind the skip. Check over the road. Recognize the house? We saw it from the lane last time. Looks pretty quiet at the moment.

Problem is, I'm starting to get this feeling.

I know they brought her here. Everything tells me they brought her here. Just as everything tells me there's eyes watching for me. I don't feel threatened yet and the car's ready to roar off the moment I sniff shit. But like I say, I'm getting this feeling.

That Jaz isn't here.

The door opens—and it's that gobbo from last night.

Riff.

39

It's no mistake. I only saw him in the dark but I caught him good enough. Got a better view now though.

One dimpy slug. About twenty, face like a thud. Heavy build but clumsy, lazy. You can see it all over him. He's no trouble, a total muffin. But he's not alone.

There's another gobbo coming out with him. I can guess who he is from his face—Trixi's brother. What did Bex call him?

Dig.

That's it. Twenty years old, she said, same as Slugchops. You don't want to cross him, she said. But I don't need telling. I can see that from his face too.

It's got Trixi's grime all over it. Different kind of dreg to Riff. Can't believe I've never seen him before. But there you go. Even with all my watching, I miss stuff.

They're moving down the road, slow, easy. Don't looked choked about anything. Certainly not sniping around for trouble. But I am. I'm watching for them and I'm watching for the others.

Still can't see anything. But they're here, Bigeyes. I told you, they're here. I can feel 'em squeezing my heart. Look back at the two gobbos.

They've stopped by a car. No checking around. They just get in like everything's no sweat. Riff's in the driver's seat. Starts up the engine.

I turn the screwdriver in the ignition switch—then stop.

Too soon to start up. Too dangerous. The other eyes watching'll make the connection with Riff's car starting and mine straight after. They'll fix on me right up.

Give it a couple more seconds. Can't give it longer or I'll lose 'em. They're heading down toward the main road. I'm itching to start up. I want to keep 'em in view. Check around. Still no sign of any eyes.

But they're there, Bigeyes. I'm telling you, they're there. There's stuff even I can't see. Only now we got to go. Can't leave it any longer or Riff'll be gone.

Twist the screwdriver. Engine fires. Check around again. Nothing moving in the driveway apart from a kid riding his trike on the pavement.

Go.

First gear, hand brake, clutch up, ease off down the road. Riff's turned right and gone but I should see him when I hit the main road. On down the driveway, and then I hear it.

The sound of another engine behind me.

Check the mirror. No sign of anyone pulling out. There's parked cars both sides of the street. Can't see which one it is. Drive on, got to drive on.

Reach the main road. Still nothing to see in the mirror. Riff's moving down toward the city center but he's caught in the slow lane. Check the mirror again.

Still nothing.

But I heard the engine. I definitely heard it. I can still hear it—I think.

Look ahead, search for an opening in the traffic. Here's one. Into the gap, turn right after Riff. He's moving faster now, five cars between us, but I got him fixed. Check back.

Still nothing there.

But they're coming, Bigeyes. I just know it. They're coming for us. I reach into my pocket, squeeze the knife.

Sound of a horn to the right. I've drifted off my lane. Let go of the knife, snap hold of the wheel, jerk left. A van slips out of my blind spot, red-haired gobbo at the wheel. Peers over at me, gives a finger, cruises past.

I'm shivering again, Bigeyes, like I was in the stream.

I got to focus, got to stay calm, got to drive good.

"Put the knife away."

That's right. Talk aloud.

"Put it away. You don't need it yet. Time later. Right now you got to drive. And you got to watch."

Traffic's speeding up again. I can still see Riff ahead. He's moving to the right lane, like he wants to turn off at the next lights.

Check mirror, move to the same lane.

Just two cars between us now and still nothing behind. Nothing that looks dangerous anyway. Just cars, cars, cars. But they're all dangerous, Bigeyes. Any one of 'em could be carrying the gobbos who want me.

And the gobbo I want in return.

But it's not just Paddy. There's something more precious I want too.

Sirens!

Shit, Bigeyes, don't tell me. . . .

They're some way back. Can't see any lights in the mirror but there's cars pulling to the side to make room. Riff's turning right at the lights. They're on green. He's heading down toward the docks. Sirens getting louder. I can see a flashing light now, still a good way back.

It's porkers. I knew it. And I'm guessing they're for me. I'm sure someone's seen me. But I'm not hanging around to find out. I got to follow Riff anyway. Why aren't the cars in front moving?

Christ! The guy behind Riff's stalled. Riff's gone on and the rest of us are stuck here. And the lights are going to change any moment.

More sirens. There's two cars at least. I can see one and hear the other. They're stuck too now, can't move cos of a truck taking up too much room, but they'll be clear the moment it shifts.

Cars in front of me are moving again, turning right one by one. Revs, clutch up, slip forward, but now the lights are turning red. Stuff it, I'm going. Can't lose Riff, whatever the risk.

Blare of horns from the oncoming cars. I'm halfway across the other lane and there's guys leaning out of car windows screaming at me. And then I'm around and racing for the docks.

Only Riff's disappeared.

Got to think, Bigeyes. There's all these turns he could have taken. I'm just praying he's carried straight on. We'll have to chance it. The road twists a bit, so he might still be hidden just ahead.

Foot down, speed up. Never mind the limit now. Got to take a risk. The old motor's groaning. Doesn't like this rattling about. At least with me jumping the lights there's a chance of throwing off the nebs who were following.

But somehow I don't think I'm that lucky. And they'll all have seen which way I went. They'll know I'm somewhere near the docks.

There's Riff. Dead ahead, see? Taking his time like the world's going to wait for him. Or is he waiting for me?

I only just thought of that.

Is he waiting for me?

He doesn't look like a smart gobbo. Nor does his mate. Hard but not smart. I don't think they've sniffed me. But there's the sirens again. And they're coming this way.

Riff's turning left down Riverside Lane.

I'm going straight on. Got to shoot clever here. Mustn't give 'em any idea they're being followed. I can take the next road and end up at the same place as Riverside Lane. Cos all these roads end up at the same place.

The docks.

Yeah, I know. Water again, effing bloody water. And this is deep stuff, big river stuff, not some spitty little stream. There's cargo ships put in here, load, unload and then haul off back to the sea. I try and keep away from this place.

But there's nothing I can do about that now.

Check the mirror. No porkers in view but lots of other cars coming after me. I want to look back, flick over the faces in 'em, but there's no time. I got to turn.

Left, down Maple Street, and there's the water at the bottom like an inky gob. I feel like I'm driving down a tunnel straight into it. I can see the sides of the street, the warehouses on either side rising over me.

And here's the wharf opening up. Warehouses drop back. Stop the car, check about me. Riff's motor's over to the left, parked outside the Dockside Diner. Dronky-looking hole if ever there was one.

They're going in.

Let 'em get out of sight, edge the car around to the right,

park by the timber merchant, get out. Rain's still coming down. Funny—I almost stopped noticing it while I was driving here. Hood up, get ready to go—and there's that feeling again.

Eyes watching.

Why can't I see 'em, Bigeyes? I don't miss stuff. I'm quick, I'm smart. Only I'm missing this. What's happening?

Face down, over to the diner, check through the window. Crowded with nebs. Men mostly, but a few women too—and a kid. Little girl, sweet face, sitting with an old guy at the far end.

But it's not the girl I'm looking for.

Riff's at the corner table rolling a cig. Dig's ordering something from the gobbo behind the counter. And now I've seen something else.

It's not what I came here for. But maybe it's what I need.

Tammy and Sash heading for the diner.

40

GOT TO MOVE, got to be in place ahead of 'em.

Into the diner. I'm glad about the crowd. It swallows me up. Can't keep my hood up though. Looks suspicious. The change of clothes, the hat, the cropped hair with its new color—that'll help a bit. But I got to use all my skill as well.

This isn't like lifting wallets in Café Blue Sox. There's nebs here who want to stiff me. But I'm okay so far. I'm hemmed around by hefty gobbos. Check about me, slow, cute.

Tammy and Sash are in the doorway. They won't go for the counter. They'll head straight over to Riff's table. Don't ask me how I know. Dig's there too now with a tray of pastries and chocolate.

Check the nearest table. Nobody sitting there but there's stuff from the last people waiting to be cleared away—two empty coffee mugs and a half-eaten roll. Grab the roll and one of the mugs. Check again.

The two trolls are still in the doorway. Tammy's bent over a cig trying to get her lighter to flash. Sash is standing with her, looking around.

Glances my way, then back at Tammy.

Did she see me, Bigeyes? Don't think so. She'd have come straight over if she had, or looked hard at me, or said something. She's not subtle enough to act like she hasn't noticed anything. She's not looking back, not speaking or anything.

Tammy's still trying to light her cig. Gobbo behind the

counter tells her no smoking. She glares at him, puts the cig and lighter away, glares at him again.

I'm pretty sure I'm okay.

I got to take the risk anyway, got to do it now.

Shuffle over toward the corner table. Got to be as spiky as I've ever been. They can't hurt me in here but I'm still stuffed if they recognize me. And it'll ruin everything I've come to do.

Table next to 'em's taken, two gobbos and a woman. Just as well. Can't sit too close. Next table's got a bearded gobbo at it. Old guy, wrinkled and smelly, reading the paper. I sit down opposite him, back to Riff and Dig. Grizzlebeard glances up at me, sniffs, looks back at his paper.

I put the roll and mug to my mouth, make like I'm eating and drinking. Behind me I hear the gobbos and the woman talking at the next table. Then, on the other side of 'em, Tammy's voice.

"Give us some money for a coffee."

Dig answers. I just know it's him. Something about the voice. Too dangerous for Riff.

"You ain't supposed to be here."

"It's cold on that hulk."

Hulk. Hear that, Bigeyes? She said hulk. Dig again.

"I don't care."

I hate this voice. There's something about it that chills me. Low, slow, like it doesn't need to shout or hurry cos it knows it's going to be obeyed.

"I told you to stay. Both of you."

"Xen and Kat are looking after 'er."

"Needs all four of you."

"No, it don't. She ain't no problem."

"Needs all four of you."

I'm thinking fast, Bigeyes. There's only so many ships and boats along the quay. Two or three of 'em could be called hulks. But there's more boats farther down the river, and some of 'em are real wrecks. Not like they're sunk but they're not safe. They've been shoved out of the way to rot and nobody's got around to sorting 'em.

But they're snugs for some of the dross around this city—if you're into sleeping in a sieve. Question is—do I wig it now and go looking or hang about in case I hear a bit more? Sash pipes up.

"We'll go back."

"Good girl," says Dig.

"Good girl," says Riff.

Yeah, yeah. Hear that, Bigeyes? What did I tell you? He's weak as piss, that Riff. Good girl, good girl. All he can manage is an echo of his mate.

"Nobody asked your opinion," Sash snaps at him.

Think she agrees with me.

"Shut it," says Dig.

She shuts it. But Tammy keeps on.

"Give us some money for a coffee and we'll go."

"I give you some already this morning. What happened to that?"

"Ain't got none left. We had to buy milk and stuff. Come on, Digs."

"All right, all right." Sound of coins dropping on the table. "But it's drink up quick and back to the *Sally Rose*."

I stiffen.

Sally Rose.

Now, she really is a hulk. But I got what I need. All I want now is for Tammy and Sash to take as long as they want over their coffee.

I keep my head down over the roll and mug. Grizzlebeard's glancing at me again. I give him a wink and he looks quickly down. Out of the corner of my eye I see Sash heading for the counter. Scrape of a chair behind me.

I'm guessing Tammy's sat down but I don't want to look.

I put down the roll and mug, stand slowly up, back to the table. I'm facing Sash now. She's standing in the queue by the counter and if she looks this way, I could be in trouble. She didn't recognize me last time but that means nothing.

Head down, slip past her, out the door.

Hood up against the rain and I'm hurrying around the front of the diner. Glance up at the window. No one watching from the corner table. Dig and Riff are leaning together, talking. Tammy's turned to shout something at Sash.

I'm gone.

Sally Rose.

One battered old tramp. Don't know what kind of cargo she carried in her working days. All she carries now is whatever duffs happen to be dossing there. I've never been much interested in who they were before.

But things are different now.

Past the derricks, past the busy end of the wharf, past the newer warehouses toward the old, deserted ones. Nothing much lives here, Bigeyes. All that moves is the river and we both know what I think of that.

Look about you. As dronky a dump as you'll find. It's a disease, this place. Water on the left, wasteland on the right—no trees, bushes, hedges, just scrawny grass and the carcasses of warehouses.

Can't see anyone following but that could change any moment. I got to keep checking. Can't stop for a second. There's enemies everywhere, even if I can't see 'em.

I'm checking the boats too. The decent ones are moored out in the river, the slaggy ones up against the bank. Couple of good'uns close in but the rest are trash, barges and lighters mostly, rotting on their lines.

And here's *Sally Rose.*

Stop, check behind. Still no sign of trouble. Nobody on the path, nobody on the water, nobody around the derelict warehouses. Reach into my pocket, feel for the knife.

Xen and Kat.

I can handle them. As long as it's just them.

I squeeze the knife and there's that shudder again. Never used to be like that, Bigeyes. Used to be simple. Blade out and do it.

But I can't stop now. I got to go through with it. I'll be all right once I've started. The old habits'll kick in. I just got to make myself do it.

Walk on, fast, quiet, watching cute.

No movement anywhere, just the river licking past. I'm trying not to look at it. Plank from the stern reaching over to the path. Dodgy-looking thing and I'm not mad about walking down it with water underneath. But there's no time to hunt for something better.

It's got to be now.

Check around. Still no sign of anyone. Onto the plank, step forward. Bounces but it's okay. Don't look at the water, just eyes on the plank and keep walking, step, step, step.

I'm on deck.

Look around me. Nobody. Got to move soft now, dead

soft. Listen hard. No voices, footsteps, no sounds at all. Hatchway on the other side, already open. Creep over, peer through.

All dark but a ladder stretching down into the boat.

Climb over, slow, quiet, ease myself down rung by rung to the bottom. I'm in the hold, darkness all around, but I'm starting to see clearer, I'm starting to hear voices.

Just a murmur but enough. It's the other two trolls. They're in a cabin somewhere in the bows. Can't hear what they're saying but I recognize the voices.

Creep forward. I don't want the trolls. I just want Jaz. But if I got to fight, I will. And you know what's scaring me now, Bigeyes?

Me.

That's right. I'm scaring myself. Cos I can feel that anger coming back. I can feel myself breathing blood again. And you know why? Cos I'm suddenly seeing it clear. It's not just Paddy that's wrong.

It's everything that's wrong.

That's what's getting to me. Everything's wrong.

Rubbing out Bex was wrong. Nicking Jaz was wrong. All that's happened to me since the day I was born—all that was wrong. All that's still wrong.

And there's part of me that wants Xen and Kat to come out. I'm squeezing the knife and I want 'em to come out. I want 'em to find me.

Cos they're wrong too. You listening to this, Bigeyes? They're wrong too. And if I can't have Paddy and all the others, I'll have them.

I'm up in the bows now and there's closed doors in front of me. The one on the right's got a taper of light around the edge. I can hear the trolls talking inside. But straight ahead's another door.

No light around the edge—just a bolt on the outside.

Drawn across.

The voices are still murmuring in the other cabin. Then suddenly they stop. But I don't care. It's too late now. And like I told you, I almost want 'em to find me. I draw back the bolt, open the door, gasp.

She's lying in the darkness, tied, gagged, eyes peering out at me from her battered face. But it's not Jaz.

"Bex," I murmur.

41

Everything happens fast now.

The other door flies open. Xen and Kat jump out, knives drawn. Thump of footsteps on the deck above, wail of sirens far down the quay. I turn to face the trolls. They're keeping back, waiting for the others probably.

"We know who you are," says Kat. "Whatever you done to your hair and clothes."

I don't answer. I'm watching 'em close but I can hear Bex behind me. She's crawled as far as the door. I reach back with the knife, cut the ropes around her wrists.

"Untie the rest," I tell her.

And I'm watching the trolls again.

I can't take my eyes off 'em for a second. More footsteps above. They haven't come down yet. Maybe they don't know I'm here. Xen screams up.

"He's down 'ere!"

Voices above, sound of running.

I feel Bex pluck at my arm. I glance back. She's untied and ungagged herself and she's crouched there behind me. Her face is a mess. Nothing broken as far as I can see but they trimmed her up proper.

"I thought you were dead," I mutter.

"Guy who killed Trixi knocked me out."

"I heard him say he killed you."

"He probably thought he did. He hit me hard enough. But

I come to. And 'e was gone and Riff was standing there with Jaz. Then Dig turned up. You can guess the rest."

So Paddy was boasting to his mates. All that stuff about killing her and dumping the body. But she hasn't done much better since.

"Who did that to your face?"

"The girls."

"Keep behind me," I say.

Shadows in the hold now. Dig, Tammy, Sash, Riff. All got knives out except Riff. But they're not rushing me. They're spreading out.

"He's still got Trixi's knife," says Xen. "See?" She calls out to Dig. "Be careful. He knows how to throw it."

"So what?" says Dig.

And he flings his own knife, not at me but at a crate nearby. The blade thuds into the wood and the shaft quivers in the dark. He watches it for a moment, then pulls out another knife, a bigger one.

"Blade," he murmurs in that slow voice. "Guy told us your name. We was hoping you'd show up again." He glances at his knife. "So we can do right by Trixi."

"I didn't kill her," I say. "The guy who spoke to you—"

"Told us everything," says Dig. "Nice polite gentleman, most obliging. Though you wouldn't want to get on the wrong side of him, I'm guessing. Or his mates. He come and found us at Tammy's gran's. Said he'd seen Trix and the girls there once before when he was looking for you."

"He's a liar."

"Said he saw you kill her. And it's not the first time you killed neither. Said him and his mates have been looking for you for years and it's time for revenge. So we all went looking for you. Put the word around to a few friends too. Kept in touch by mobile. Riff found you on the lane and rang us. Rest was easy. Or should have been. We done our bit. They cocked up theirs. But here you are anyway."

"I didn't kill Trixi. Paddy did. The guy you spoke to. Bex was there. Ask her."

"Yeah, like we're going to believe a word she says." Dig scowls at her. "She's never said nothing true all her life. That's why I'm finished with her."

I glance at Bex again. She's staring at me with this haunted look. She nods suddenly.

"He's right. Him and me, we was . . ."

She falls silent. I look back at Dig.

"Yeah," he says. "We was. Only we ain't now."

So that's how Bex got in the gang. It wasn't cos she was tough. I knew that anyway. It was cos she was Dig's girl.

My mind's starting to spin. I got to stop it, got to keep my head, got to remember what I came here for. I square up to Dig.

"Where's Jaz?"

He raises his eyebrow. "Jaz?"

"Where is she?"

"You want Jaz, do you?" He glances at the others, chuckles. "He wants Jaz."

They chuckle too. He turns back, studies me with a leer.

"I don't think Jaz'll want you. Not looking like that. You seen your face lately?"

"Where is she?"

"She ain't going to want nothing to do with you." He lowers his voice. "Cos you look scary, boy. You're so angry you're spitting flames. You got a rage in your head like I never seen. It don't freak me out. But it's going to freak her."

I'm trembling, Bigeyes. Cos I know he's right. I'm breathing blood worse than ever. But I can still do it. I can calm myself for Jaz. And she'll trust me. She's that kind of kid. She trusts. She'll know it's me.

I got to get her away. Her and Bex. Dig's no father for her. She needs her mum. And she needs me. Whatever it takes, I got to get her away.

"Let me see her," I say.

Dig gives me a smirk, then nods toward a door on the far side of the hold.

"Feel free," he says. "But don't say I didn't warn you."

I look around at them all. They're watching me close, watching the knife in my hand. For all their numbers and Dig's bravado, they're scared of what I can do. I stare at the far door.

"Move back," I say.

I see eyes flicker toward Dig. He nods. They move back, still watching me. I reach behind me, feel for Bex's hand. She takes it, holds it tight.

I lead her across the hold to the other side. No one moves, speaks. All's quiet, just the creak of the hull and the drumming of the rain on the deck above.

I reach the door, let go Bex's hand, check around at the others. They're still standing there watching. I look back at the door. No taper of light but no bolt across either. If she's in here, she's no prisoner. Unless she's tied up.

I open the door.

And there she is. She's sitting on a little box facing out. She's got a pencil in one hand and a drawing book in the other, clasped to her chest. She staring out with wide eyes. They fix on me, recognize me. I smile, murmur.

"Jaz, it's me, baby."

She opens her mouth and screams.

It stuns me. I never heard a sound like it, never from her, never from anyone. Cos I never heard fear like it before. And I can't bear it. Cos I know it's what Dig said. It's fear of my anger, fear of my face, fear of me.

"Jaz, it's okay. It's me. It's—"

She screams again, louder.

"Jaz, I'm not going to hurt you."

More screams. She's turning her face, twisting her body, like she wants to block me out. I lean in, touch her arm.

She jerks it away like I've scalded her.

"Jaz, listen." I'm murmuring, whispering, desperate to reach her, desperate to break through her terror. "Jaz, I've come to look after you. I got money and a car to get us away. You and me and Bex. We're going to be all right."

I'm talking wild, promising the earth. It was the plan—the money, the car, the escape. It's not going to happen now with Dig and the others here but I keep talking anyway, keep trying to make her smile at me.

"Jaz, Jaz. . . ."

She just screams again and again, then scrambles to the farthest side of the cabin, presses herself against the hull, hands over her ears, face dipped so she can't see me. I feel Bex pull me back, thrust the door shut. From inside the cabin the screams go on.

The others are moving close again.

"So this is where it all ends," says Dig. "And luckily I don't have to get my hands dirty. There's others to do that for us."

He glances around at Riff, who's talking quietly on a mobile.

I'm still reeling. My mind won't work. All I can think of is Jaz's screams, her face, her total terror—of me. I can't take that, Bigeyes. Not terror of me. Not Jaz. And suddenly it's like nothing else matters anymore.

Only that's not right. There's still Bex. She still matters, even if I don't.

"Let Bex go," I say. "Do what you want with me. Only let Bex go. And let her take her kid."

"I would," says Dig. He pauses. "If she had a kid."

Silence. A deep, scary silence. Rain's stopped. So have the screams. I make myself speak.

"You telling me . . . ?"

"Ask Bex."

I look around at her and there's that haunted face again.

"Tell me the truth," I say.

"I love that kid," she mutters.

"Tell me the truth."

"We was good mates. We still is. We bonded cos I looked after her at Tammy's gran's. We're like dead close. There's nobody in the world she trusts more than me. And she's got no father. Ask Dig. The guy legged it. One-night stand and gone."

"You haven't told me what I need to know."

Another silence. I bellow at her in the dark, echoing shell.

"Who's Jaz's mother?"

She looks down, whispers.

"Trixi."

42

I SEE DIG STEP FORWARD. He's got trolls either side of him. They're like shadows now, all of 'em. I can't even see their eyes. But maybe I'm not looking. Cos somehow I don't care anymore. No point in caring, no point in anything.

Jaz doesn't want me. And Bex is a dreg.

The shadows stop. Dig leans closer.

I see the big knife start to move. It hews the darkness as it gathers pace. I see my thoughts scatter before it, pricking my mind with tiny screams. Duck, they tell me. Dodge, parry, do something. There's time.

I know there is. I've been here before. But I don't move. I just watch, my own knife dead in my hand.

I feel a hot pain as the blade scores my brow. Blood fills my eyes and I fall to the floor. I hear screams, Becky first, then Jaz behind the door. Then I'm screaming too.

I hear the trolls start to yell, feel 'em crowd around. Then the kicks come thudding in. I curl up into a ball. A hand grabs my hair, yanks my head up.

I'm staring through the blood into Dig's face. I'm still holding Trixi's knife. I want to stab it right through him but I can't move and he knows it.

He gives a grin, then suddenly I'm jerked up on my feet and he's bundling me through the darkness. The trolls are still packed around me, punching, kicking, scratching, but I don't notice 'em now, don't notice anything, just the ladder thrust against my eyes.

And I'm scrambling up, Dig's knife prodding me on, and then I'm out on deck and the rain's drizzling down again, and I'm staring about me, trying to think. But my mind's split open and I'm fumbling through a fog.

Dig's on deck now, and the trolls, and they're closing around me again, kicking and shoving me toward the plank. I blunder over it onto the bank and stagger down the path.

They don't follow. They're still on the *Sally Rose,* jeering at me. And somehow I can hear Jaz's screams again. Maybe they're inside my head. I don't know. All I know is that she doesn't want me.

I turn and totter down the bank. Blood's flowing worse now and my head's thumping. I know I'm badly hurt. I see porkers down the path, checking out the wharf. But they're the least of my problems.

There's two gobbos climbing out of the nearest barge. I recognize 'em. Lenny and the grunt. They've obviously been keeping out of sight of the porkers while they wait for me to show up.

Check around.

Third gobbo coming up behind, fourth to his left covering the waste ground, fifth climbing out of a lighter farther down.

No sign of Paddy.

But what does that matter now, Bigeyes? It's all over anyway. I'm never going to get Paddy before they get me. Cos I'm finished, you understand? I'm totally effing finished. I can still run a bit but where to? Where can I go? I got a hundred yards in me, maybe two.

Even if I wanted to give myself up to the porkers, I couldn't reach 'em. They're too far away, they haven't seen me and I got no voice left to shout.

I got one choice left, just one. That crumbly old warehouse. Probably won't get there before they catch me and even if I do, there's nowhere much to hide. But what else can I do?

Run, run.

Only it isn't a run. It's a lurch. I'm hurting bad in the head now and the blood's rushing down my face. I still got the knife but it feels useless, as useless and spent as I am.

Look back.

They're coming after me, all five. Not hurrying. Why should they? They know I can't get far. Shuffle over the scraggy grass, through the entrance to the warehouse.

Like I told you, nowhere much to hide. But if I can just get across the storage room and out the far window before they see me, they might think I've gone into one of the old offices.

Trouble is, I'm struggling bad now and the blood's making it hard to see. But I'm halfway over the storage room and still no sign of the gobbos. Few more yards and . . .

The window.

Shattered long ago, thank God, and beyond it the waste ground on the other side of the building. Check around. Gobbos not here yet but they won't be far away.

Squeeze into the window, slow, heavy. I'm moving like a dead weight, grazing my legs on the spikes of glass still left in the frame. Then suddenly I'm through and outside again.

Only I can't move. I'm slumped against the wall, I'm pouring blood, and I can't get up.

I hear sounds on the other side of the wall, footsteps moving about the storage room. Hard to tell how many of 'em are in there. I don't give two bells anyway. Nothing I can do anymore. I'm not going to make it even if they don't find me.

But they have found me.

There's a figure walking this way.

Easy one to recognize. My old friend the grunt. He's come around the outside of the building and he's strolling down toward me, nice and easy, nice and slow.

Yeah, that's right. No need to rush now, big guy. Just as well cos you're not that fit, are you? You're all on your own and I can see right into your mind. Even with my head drummed, I can read your little brain.

You're thinking, I don't need to call the others. I'll sort the kid on my own.

He's close now and you know what, Bigeyes? I'm clutching the knife and I'm wondering. He's moved away from the wall to skirt those nettles and now he's walking toward me.

Straight on.

I couldn't miss him if I wanted to. He's the biggest, fattest target in the world. I still got the strength, just. One throw and he's down. Easy, easy.

Does he know how much danger he's in?

Obviously not cos he's coming straight on. I squeeze the hilt, finger the blade, whip my arm back ready. He stops. He's just a few yards away but if he moves, he's a dead man. And he knows it now.

I call out to him.

"Where's Paddy, fat man?"

I don't expect an answer. But he gives me one in that thick, grunty voice.

"Helping the police with their inquiries."

Christ, Bigeyes. They got him after all. I never thought that would happen. Least my tip-off did something. But I still wish I'd killed him. The grunt sniffs.

"Ain't going to help you much though."

He's right. There's figures appearing both sides now. The other gobbos. They walk slowly around and stare down at me. I'm still holding the knife ready.

"Go on, then, kid," says Lenny. "Throw it."

I want to, Bigeyes. I want to throw it so bad. Only I can't. I'm streaming blood and I'm crying. Crying for Jaz, crying for me, crying for everything that's never going to be.

I see 'em step forward but it's all a blur now. I don't know what's happening anymore. I feel the knife twisted out of my hand, feel 'em poke through my pockets, pull out the money, joke, laugh.

Then the blow. It shatters the light, drowns my head. As I slip into the dark, I see Lenny lean toward me. Suddenly there's a crack—a sharp, heavy sound I've heard before.

Only I'm not thinking, Bigeyes, I'm not right. Everything's jumbled, everything's mad. Another crack. And this time I recognize it.

Gunfire.

Have I been shot? I don't know, Bigeyes. Cos nothing makes sense now. I can't feel my body. I'm drifting like breath through a murky space. I don't know who I am, where I am, what I am. But I hear a voice—low, distant.

"Blade," it says.

I know it right away.

Mary.

"But you're dead," I murmur. "You got shot in the bungalow. And you don't know my name. I never told you."

She doesn't answer. But I see her face in the darkness. It's like she's floating with me in this misty place. And now there's more faces. They're floating too, all around me. Faces from the past, faces I don't want to see.

Enemies.

And I'm looking back at Mary and wondering.

"Are you an enemy too?"

Again she doesn't answer. The faces go on floating, floating, floating. Then one by one they start to slip away. And that's when I get it, Bigeyes. That's when I understand. They're from the past. But they're not the past.

They're the future.

That's right. If I live through this, they'll come back.

But for now they're slipping away. Like me. Fading into nothing. And you know what, Bigeyes? Maybe that's best.

Cos if I'm nothing, they can't ever hurt me again.